GW00399933

Scribe Publications
THE PORTRAIT

WILLEM JAN OTTEN, who was born in 1951, is a multi-award-winning Dutch poet, essayist, playwright, and novelist. His novel *The Portrait*, published in Holland as *Specht en zoon* ('Specht and Son'), was awarded that country's prestigious literary award, the Libris Literary Prize, in 2005.

DAVID COLMER was born in Adelaide in 1960. Since moving to Amsterdam in the early 1990s, he has published a wide range of translations of Dutch literature. He is also a published author of fiction, and in 2009 was awarded the biennial NSW Premier's Translation Prize.

For Kees Otten, my father

THE
PORTRAIT
—
WILLEM
JAN
OTTEN

Translated by David Colmer

SCRIBE

Melbourne • London

Scribe Publications Pty Ltd
18–20 Edward St, Brunswick, Victoria 3056, Australia
50A Kingsway Place, Sans Walk, London, EC1R 0LU, United Kingdom

Published in Australia and New Zealand by Scribe 2009
Reprinted 2013
This edition published 2014

First published as *Specht en zoon* by G.A. van Oorschot 2005

This edition has been published with the financial support of the Foundation
for the Production and Translation of Dutch Literature.

Typeset in Adobe Caslon Pro by the publishers
Printed and bound in England by CPI Group (UK) Ltd.

National Library of Australia
Cataloguing-in-Publication data

Otten, Willem Jan.

The Portrait.

9781921372469 (Australian edition)
9781922247537 (UK edition)
9781925113266 (e-book)

Portrait painters-Fiction.

A823.3

scribepublications.com.au
scribepublications.co.uk

Note on Pronunciation

The Dutch letter-combination of 'ij'—found in this book in the names Lidewij, Tijn, and Stijn—is equivalent to the English 'i' or 'y'. These three names can be pronounced *Lee-de-why*, *Tine*, and *Stine*.

ONE

I'm coming to a tragic end; that seems almost certain now. The sliding doors are open. I can hear fire raging; it crackles. The wind is blowing directly from the north and into the studio. Sparks shoot towards me, turn to ash, and drift in like flakes of snow. I am on the easel and can only expect the worst.

He walks in from the garden. He's coming to get me. There's no doubt anymore. He's going to throw me on the fire.

I'm telling you this now, right at the start, because otherwise you'll close the book the moment you realise who I am, inevitably thinking, What's *he* going to experience?

Getting a bit loose maybe ... or having a lamp with a sharp edge fall over against him during a cleaning session, and then he gets a dent ... at worst, a tear. And in the long run — come on, what can existence possibly have in store for him? Ending up in an attic, with his front against the back of someone else who has also been taken down off the wall ... Not a cheerful prospect, true, but in the meantime he'll have done his thing, for at least the span of a human life. Fulfilling his task and carrying to the best of his ability whatever is depicted on him.

For heaven's sake, what can be tragic about someone who is only a support?

That's what they call us in the trade. Supports.

One painter will sometimes ask another, What kind of support do you work on?

Double-weave linen, the other replies. Or portrait linen, when I'm working small format.

Ah, the first says. I swear by extra fine.

They can debate the subject with all the detail that wine lovers bring to discussions of different vintages.

What's ideal about double weave is the structure, the resistance to the brush, like licking an orange.

That's the kind of thing I heard them say, and they seemed to understand each other. I pricked up my ears because, when it comes down to it, listening has always been my only way of finding out who or what I am. I mean, if you, like me, come into the world white and completely blank, with nothing on you at all, you are totally dependent on what they make of you. That's what makes the little they say about you while you are still unpainted so tremendously important.

Like everyone else, I started as a roll, hanging between the other rolls at Van Schendel's. I remember virtually nothing of that hanging. We are going to spend our whole life hanging, but our first hanging remains a mystery. I was somewhere in the middle of the roll, in suffocating, unconscious darkness. The shop assistants called our roll a *two metre*, because of our width. There were other rolls called *one-and-a-halfs*. Most canvases by far were cut out of them. I don't know when exactly the two-metre-wide roll containing me was hung up at Van Schendel's. All of that is prehistory, as far back in my past as an ovum in a human's. That's why I have no idea how long it took for the section of roll I would be cut out of to reach me. It could have been years. I do know that I spent almost ten months with some sixty centimetres of my surface hanging out into the shop, like a dog's tongue. Several times, a shop assistant rolled me out a little further to let a customer look at me and, above all, feel me — then he rolled me back up again.

I am an Extra Fine Quadruple Universal Primed. Anyone who wanted to look at me more closely knew I cost a fortune, especially compared to the One-and-a-Half Double Weave to my right, which, although Oil Primed, had, according to the customers and shop assistants, a significantly shorter staple.

The problem with the roll I come from was size. Two metres is the maximum width, but my quality was close to the highest imaginable. Do you see the rub? Unusually large formats could be cut out of me, but almost none of the artists working in those formats painted with the precision my quality actually demands. Your format, as my final owner would say, is more daubed than painted.

I'm not going to say I despaired in the year I spent rolled out to the daylight like a sheet of toilet paper. More than just waiting, I learnt to daydream. I let myself be carried away by fantasies about who would finally want me. Who in this country was famous enough to afford me? Because that was what my daydreams always came down to: my painter *had* to be a prestigious artist, otherwise he could never afford me. No wonder that I, despite my innate modesty, began to fantasise about life in a gallery, with visitors thronging around me every day.

Absurd, because people who paint precisely enough to want me invariably produce work that trend-setting art lovers and the curators of the temples of contemporary art write off as old-fashioned.

Pandering. Kitsch.

I admit to remembering virtually nothing of the moment I was finally bought. It was a nondescript man, smallish, in a dark-blue army-disposals coat and paint-splashed shoes. He had wide, avid eyes, but I didn't really see them while the transaction was taking place. During purchases they don't actually look at you from the front; instead they feel you and look at you from the side to see how the light catches your surface. One prospective buyer even licked me — before going back to the One-and-a-Half Double Weave next to me, which she had only felt with the inside of her wrist, as if testing a baby's bottle. As if Double Weave has a special temperature ... It simply didn't occur to me that the man in the blue coat was seriously considering me — he looked so unrenowned. I didn't even interrupt my daydreaming, and only woke with a start after he had turned and was striding off, gesticulating and talking away to Dennis, who always worked in Van Schendel's on Wednesdays. At the counter he began to order me.

Two metres by a hundred and twenty. Wooden frame, six-centimetre stretchers, with wedges, stapled not nailed. Yes, a huge format. Dennis thought so, too, and I could see that he had to do his very best not to ask what I was going to be. The man in the blue coat gestured, spreading his arms, as if to show that he was thinking of a *life-sized figure*, but who or what I couldn't make out. Huge, that word was mentioned several times and, yes, for him it was the first time it was going to be something *standing*. Absolutely, a cross at the back to reinforce the frame would be very wise. And the stretchers, shouldn't they be glued, three-point-six thick, to give it that bit of extra stability?

I couldn't see the counter from where I was hanging — the shelf with tubes of Rembrandt was in the way. But I did catch his name, or were they only his Christian names?

Felix Vincent.

It didn't ring any bells.

Maybe I thought, What kind of self-respecting artist calls himself Vincent?

My whole life long I had hung diagonally opposite a poster of furiously painted sunflowers. It was actually the only work of art I knew.

Yes, that's exactly what I thought. A serious painter wouldn't call himself Vincent. He'd know better.

I obviously had a premonition. Something wasn't right. The indescribable end, in the flames of the pyre that is now roaring so fiercely outside in the garden that I have started to feel its warmth — was that really contained in this moment?

It could have been anger as well, at myself, for suddenly feeling such a troubling sense of unease — when it was actually one of the greatest moments of my life. My purchase! My conception! The moment when someone said, I want that one! Use that to make the canvas on which I will realise my vision!

Two by a hundred and twenty, standing. That's nothing to be sneezed at.

Two weeks later, he came back to pick me up. If I had the gift of speech, I would now describe what it feels like to finally be a canvas, a canvas with dimensions, a piece of linen that has been measured out, cut with the most razorish Stanley knife and irrevocably stretched tight around a sturdy frame with six-centimetre stretchers no less than three-point-six thick, with wedges and a cross at the back.

A kite that is being flown for the first time might feel more majestic, a kettledrum about to start its premiere performance of Beethoven's Fifth might feel mightier, a newly raised mainsail filling with wind while its ship heels beneath it might feel more ecstatic — but we, the unpainted, silent and as white as chalk, enter a world that promises us more than kite, drum, or sail. Who could be more on edge with curiosity? More willing? More receptive?

When I was carried out of the shop by Felix Vincent and a young, blonde woman in an apple-green leather jacket and apple-green basketball boots—who I would later identify as the love of his life, Lidewij, Lidewij Gams—I knew there was only one creature in the world I could be compared to: a newborn babe.

Just before they came in to carry me off, out of the shop, onto the pavement, into Amsterdam, to the side street where they had parked their van, Mr van Schendel gave my wedges a final tap, and my frame groaned in all four corners as if in labour, wedge against wood, wood against wedge, stretching me one last time until I couldn't go any further. And Felix Vincent flicked my skin with his right index finger, exactly in my middle—yes, flicked is the right word, just like shooting a crumb off a table. Vincent flicked me in the middle like that, and I boomed like a Turkish drum.

I was so excited—beside myself, in fact—at being carried out into the summery street and feeling, for the first time in my existence, the sunlight splashing against my chalky-white front for the first and possibly last time—I realised that, too—that I felt like kissing the man who had chosen me, ordered me, and had now picked me up. Creator! I hummed with all my wedges. Creator! Do with me what you will! Make me someone!

He does paint people, my creator—people only. I soon discovered that, even though I was plonked down at first in a corner of his studio with my front against a fairly cold wall. Originally it must have been the outside wall of the house, but a sunroom was added on this side, more than twenty years ago now—a sunroom facing north, which doesn't get any direct sunlight until late February at around six o'clock in the evening.

Leaning against the wall here is hardly an ideal location. I noticed that when winter set in; from early October you feel the damp rising. Despite the radiators in the sunroom, it's as if this wall demands its old rights as an outside wall. If I had been a piano they definitely wouldn't have put me here.

I will continue to call him Creator, although I get the impression he doesn't really consider himself a creative artist. But he doesn't like the term 'portrait artist' either. From the conversations he sometimes has in the studio with people who are sitting for him, I gather that, for him, *portrait artist* evokes an image of a man with a felt hat, an elegantly draped scarf, and the eye of a hairdresser.

If I think about it, his most conspicuous trait is his longing to be inconspicuous.

I have come to realise that this is unusual for someone of his age. He must be in his early thirties, but looks younger because his cheeks are so smooth. He wants to be someone you would never take for an artist.

And the same goes for my work, he says. If you see one of my things, you shouldn't have to think about me for a second.

He invariably calls something he has made a *thing*.

He knows full well that this kind of talk is nonsense. Once, during a sudden clean-up that left me facing into the studio for a few hours, I got to see some of his things, and my first thought was, How is it possible? We're living in the twenty-first century—what kind of painter copies reality in such fussy detail? What kind of person is this Creator?

He finds reactions like that galling, despite his being without a doubt the most famous and best-paid portrait painter of his generation. He feels as if people don't really take him seriously, and he tries to brush it off with a joke.

People think I only record what's there, he says, like a camera with a tiny paintbrush attached. But in reality they get to see something they don't see.

They is the art mafia. The one-eyed mob who always

say that he paints oh-so skilfully, but has no style of his own. That he has no conceptual base.

It's all there in one of my things, but you still get to see something you can't see.

I've heard him say this quite a few times to interviewers, to sitters, to people who are thinking of commissioning him.

Sometimes people proved resistant to Creator's charm and profundity, and then he'd offer Jeanine as an example. That's one of his early portraits, from the mid-nineties. She still hangs in his studio. During a retrospective, they made a postcard of her — she's probably Creator's best-known thing. Jeanine was the checkout chick at a mini-supermarket in Huizen where he sometimes did his shopping. Looking at Jeanine, you immediately notice her shy, evasive expression. Is she looking at you out of the corner of her eye, or is she trying to avoid eye contact? As uncertain as the look in her eyes is the gesture she is making with her left hand. It hardly sounds possible but, if you look at the painting, you see that Creator has succeeded in conveying beyond a shadow of a doubt that Jeanine is covering something with her hand. This is the gesture of a woman who, noticing that someone is looking at her, is trying to hide something on her face.

What?

That's what you ask yourself, constantly.

What has Creator seen? Why does Jeanine want to

keep the left side of her face covered?

That's what I'm trying to say, Creator says. My things let you see what you can't see. You can't take your eyes off them, because it's all there. Get it?

Nowadays it's very unusual for him to ask someone to sit for him. People come to him, he goes from commission to commission, and every year he is able to drastically increase the price of one of his things. He generally works on three portraits simultaneously, and each portrait requires three sittings. On average, he works on a thing for three weeks. He does close to thirty paintings a year. If he keeps it up for another year he will have saved half of the enormous amount he needs to buy the house with the studio, which still belongs to Lidewij's family. As soon as her Aunt Drea is dead, her aunts and uncles will put Withernot on the market. That's the name of the house the studio is attached to.

Withernot has been in the family since the 1910s. Creator and Lidewij are only living here temporarily, with the permission of the aunts and uncles, who would rather leave the illusion of a family estate intact as long as Aunt Drea is still alive. When Lidewij's mother fell ill, four years ago now, Creator and Lidewij moved into Withernot to be close to her for the duration. After her death, they began toying with the idea of making their stay permanent.

Creator is tremendously preoccupied with calculations. I notice it because he does them out loud while working, at least when he's focused on his work—constantly half-singing, half-humming amounts, adding them up, then multiplying by two and dividing by ten, and adding the results. That's because he still thinks almost exclusively in guilders rather than euros.

At the aunts and uncles' insistence, the final asking price for Withernot will be the *real market value*, a cool one-and-a-half million guilders, and Creator is planning on *coughing up half of that* with *money he's painted together himself*. That's how he talks: while painting away, he distributes the imaginary amounts into *tax categories* or puts them away *fixed term*. And always I notice that Creator, while busily scratching numbers into his internal wallpaper, is somehow thinking of me. I can't prove it, but I feel it. I notice that, when calculating how many more commissions he has to complete to keep Withernot *out of the uncles' claws*, his thoughts return to the big, unpainted, standing canvas of two metres by one metre twenty on which he will one day make something that will take everyone by surprise.

During my first months in the studio, I listened in to one sitting after the other and discovered Creator's gift for making people curious about his special view of them. He always got people talking, and it was almost always about the very thing they were afraid he would somehow exaggerate in the painting — their birthmark, their wrinkly neck, their pudgy wrists — and although I never really worked out how he managed this, he often succeeded in turning the most feared into the most special. With my back turned to the scene, I got to know dozens of people without seeing them for a single second.

But Creator himself — he remained the great unknown. He was the tactful elicitor of the most detailed intimacies, without ever revealing anything of himself. No wonder I was often unable to control my daydreaming about his plans for me. It became a kind of craving: I was going to become something immeasurably important, something fundamentally unutterable. *Something whereof one cannot speak.* I mean, I landed in his studio, against the cold wall, when he was up to his neck in commissions; there was no question of his working on something for himself. Creator has a plan, I told myself, otherwise how could he have been so sure of my dimensions and, above all, of the fact that I was going to be *standing*. He has a plan for me, a plan that has sprung entirely from his imagination. Something he doesn't have to do for the money, or on commission, or because he just happens to be so good at capturing people …

I was going to become something hugely important.

And then, for a few seconds one afternoon, I thought I knew what Creator had in mind for me. That was late October, a little more than a year ago now. Creator and Lidewij called it an incredibly warm autumn. The trees were bare, but they kept the sliding doors open from early in the morning until late in the afternoon. Sometimes a restless breeze sprung up; I heard leaves rustling into the studio.

Creator had let someone in, and I soon realised it wasn't someone who had come to sit for him. She was called Minke. Minke Dupuis. She had come, she said, to make a portrait of him. They had to laugh at that, Creator and Minke. It turned out they knew each other from high school. Minke Dupuis worked for *Palazzo*, a glossy magazine that mainly existed to be leafed through by people who lived in large, free-standing houses, or at least by people who dreamt of living in large, free-standing houses. I'm doing it on the side, Minke said — the pay is fantastic. It was clear that the portrait Minke would write about him was in Creator's best interest, given that his work generally came to hang in large, free-standing houses. Minke sounded apologetic; she would have preferred to be doing an in-depth interview with him for *Art & Facts*, for which she also worked from time to time.

At that stage, I couldn't form an image of her. I heard her voice, which was slightly husky, a husky contralto. Creator just said she hadn't changed a bit.

And she said something similar. Lidewij had led her to the studio through the garden.

After Lidewij had left them alone together, Creator said, Weird, you here, all of a sudden. And Minke said that his eyes were that same old gruesome blue.

He sniggered and said, Look who's talking.

A silence I didn't know how to interpret followed.

So this is where you live, Minke said.

Yep, Creator replied. I'm working my fingers to the bone to buy it.

These words didn't actually break the silence.

Afterwards they disappeared into the garden where Lidewij had put out tea for them, on the round table near the reeds. There, essentially out of my earshot, they had the conversation that would lead to the portrait in *Palazzo* — about Creator, his work, how he lived, and who with. That same week, a photographer would come to take photos of the studio and Withernot.

They still ended up late that afternoon in the studio, Minke and Creator. The interview was clearly over. Minke said that she had enough material; more than enough.

Don't expect too much of it, she said.

Apparently she was looking at the things Creator was working on.

Don't you get sick to death of all these blasé characters?

Creator must have answered with a gesture.

I noticed that she was walking in my direction.

And that? Is that going to be it?

She was taking liberties; Creator's silence told me that much.

I felt myself being pulled back and saw, for a second, the female face that must have been Minke. And I felt her hair brushing over me, more or less where, if I became someone, my face would be.

Long, auburn hair. But her eyes weren't gruesome blue. They were dark green.

I haven't started yet, Creator said.

I noticed, Minke replied. She let go of me and I fell back against the wall, wafting her hair up away from me.

I'd rather it wasn't in the interview, Creator said.

God, no, she said. *Palazzo* readers aren't interested in something like that.

She sounded extra husky, and there was a clearly mocking undertone to her voice.

I meant it ironically, Creator said.

As far as I could tell, they said goodbye without touching. Minke said that the portrait would be in the December issue.

Don't expect too much of it.

After she had disappeared, Lidewij entered the studio from the garden. She was sliding the glass door shut when Creator came in from the house.

You never told me that, Lidewij said. That you were planning that for that big canvas.

Were you eavesdropping?

I just happened to hear. I was on the other side of the garden; the bulbs need planting, Lidewij said. Wasn't I supposed to hear it or what?

A silence fell.

It's not going to happen anytime soon anyway, Creator said.

That's not what I mean, she said. It's just strange you never mentioned it.

Creator sounded irritated.

We don't need to tell each other everything we're planning.

You don't have to tell me anything, but why tell it all of a sudden to a complete stranger who's come to interview you?

Minke's not a complete stranger. We were in sixth form together.

It was easy to hear that Lidewij was trying not to sound jealous.

Why don't you tell me things like that?

The plan sucks, Creator said. It's nonsense. That's why I told her. So I'd realise it's nonsense. Genuine, god-awful nonsense.

I think Lidewij was shocked by his tone.

I'm an idiot, too, he said. A Pietà—I just blurted something out, and that bimbo took it seriously. No sense of irony whatsoever. Anyway, she promised she wouldn't put it in the interview.

I don't know where the conversation went from there, because suddenly I was completely overcome.

A Pietà!

Meant ironically—but still, a Pietà!

I really didn't have the slightest idea of what it might be: the only works of art I had ever seen in my whole life were a few of Creator's portraits in progress and the reproduction of flaming sunflowers that had hung diagonally opposite me in Van Schendel's.

During that first phase of my existence, I found it extremely difficult to get used to the idea that we canvases are not the only supports for images. It is possible to print entire pictures on much smaller surfaces. I even discovered that a likeness of a canvas can be recorded on a minuscule, shiny support called a photo or a Polaroid.

And one day I heard a woman who was about to sit for Creator talk about a support I never really fathomed completely. She asked Creator, Do you have a reason for not having a mirror in your salon?

This woman always called the studio a salon; it seemed to annoy Creator. When she's around I feel like a beautician, he once said to Lidewij.

Yes, I have a reason, Creator replied. Here in the studio, I'm the only one who looks.

Oh, I see, the woman replied.

I have never really managed to understand exactly what a mirror is. I deduced from the rest of the conversation that, like me, a mirror can be hung, and that people then look *in* it. But what a mirror actually represents was beyond me.

It must be something fundamentally different from

what they are going to do with me, when I'm finally a painting, I thought. As far as I know, no one is ever going to look *in* me. Just *at*.

Confusing grammar. I found it a little unsettling, all the more when I realised that everyone who looks *in* the mirror sees something else. I often wondered whether I would ever understand what it was about, and it began to dawn on me that there were many things that I would never understand, simply because I didn't have any legs.

That was how I bided my time in the studio during the first and only autumn of my unpainted existence, and it became increasingly difficult for me to believe that I was ever going to amount to anything. I wasn't the only blank canvas in Withernot; in fact, there was a constant coming and going of blank canvases, always much smaller than me and always the same dimensions — ninety by seventy. They arrived by the half-dozen: modest, taciturn characters of a slightly lower quality than I, somewhere between Fine and Double Weave. They knew their fate. They would become a portrait, from just below the shoulders to the crown. They would, after their completion, be picked up relatively quickly by whoever had commissioned them; they would show a likeness first and foremost, and only then be beautiful or delightful; and they would end up in a room, on a warm wall, in a centrally heated, slightly-too-dry living room, in a life they would finally call their own.

Secretly, I pitied them: it was all so ordinary. You're ninety by seventy, Creator paints a face and shoulders on you — usually of a loving wife, or a radiant ten-year-old daughter holding a teddy bear, or, if you're lucky, of the chairman of the board of the convention centre. And through the eyes of this one face, you then view the world, hanging over a sofa, or in the curve of a staircase, or on the boardroom wall.

I knew I shouldn't think like that. My year in Van Schendel's had ennobled me and taught me to dream. I had been spared their format. But I was still uneasy. I admit it with reluctance. I had come to realise that, in the life of a canvas like me, only one thing counts. Even when you don't become a Pietà, there is still that one question: Who was going to be painted on me? Who would I become? Whose countenance would become my countenance? Yes, it's true, words like that ran through my mind. Countenance. As if it was on special. Through whose eyes would I observe the world?

I told myself a thousand times, What difference does not becoming something make if you don't even know what that thing is? But it didn't help. Ever since that warm afternoon in October, I had felt an inexplicable regret. I realised that Creator would never carry out his plan, but I had no idea why not. No more than I understood why he had ever conceived the plan in the first place.

You can't follow them, people who want to make something they don't understand. The unknown can only slip through their fingers; I understood that much. They recoil from their deepest convictions.

If I was ever to become something, one day, it would not be what was intended.

A few days later, I was dragged back from the gates of hell. Don't ask me how. Creator was asked whether he would like to paint Cindy. Yes, that's the one, the wife of Fokke Ponsen, of Procter Poldermol, with whom she would soon be celebrating their first anniversary. Once again that year, Ponsen had made it into the top ten of the Dutch rich list.

Cindy was the first facelifted person that Creator would paint.

During the first interview, when specifying the details of the commission, he tried to approach her like anyone else—but he kept getting the feeling, as he told Lidewij afterwards, that if he accepted Cindy he would *not be painting from life*. With her corrected mouth, her accentuated nostrils, her pulled-back cheeks, and her smoothed frown, it was, he said, as if Cindy was already a portrait. He was not happy about it at all, because he had already accepted the job; or, at least, he hadn't rejected it, such that it would be very awkward for him to turn it down now.

And damaging, he said, at this stage.

He meant: Now that Aunt Drea really is headed for a nursing home and we—if we want to buy

Withernot—need to make as much money as we possibly can.

In moments like these, he always said 'we'.

It seemed to me that the interview with Minke was still preying on his mind, and he kept thinking of her question—whether he got sick to death of all these blasé characters.

And then, suddenly, in Lidewij's presence, he made a decision and swore. I don't mean that he swore to do something. He started swearing and pulled me away from the wall, lifted me up by the cross at my back, turned me around, and carried me over to the easel. Lidewij was standing there and he asked her to hold me for a moment. Then he adjusted the easel so that I could stand on it, with my bottom at his knee height.

You're serious, Lidewij said.

I was standing on the easel for the first time in my life. But I felt faint at heart.

Creator shrugged. Why not?

Someone like Cindy on *that* canvas ... you must be joking, Lidewij said.

Someone like Cindy is perfect, Creator said. She's fascinating, if you really look at her. Fascinatingly mask-like.

He knew he was lying, and that made him more and more convinced that he was doing the right thing.

Cindy Ponsen from head to toe—that's cutting edge, he said.

I noticed that he hadn't looked at me for a single second, as if I already had eyes for him to look away from. All I saw was how small and nondescript he was. With me upright like this, his shoulders only came up to my middle.

Lidewij looked at me. I remembered the apple-green shoes, to which I now added her chestnut eyes. She reached out with one hand and stroked my linen with her fingertips.

Why so cynical? It's not like you.

They went for a walk through the woods around Withernot, and for the first time I was able to look out into the world at my leisure, which is to say through the sliding doors and into the garden. I was still trembling from the unutterable menace I had faced, but also from the feathery touch of Lidewij's fingertips. For a moment, it had seemed to me as if she had turned my linen into human skin.

It was early November. I know that because, while looking around the studio, I discovered a calendar on a side wall, hanging next to Jeanine, who was always just on the point of not sliding her hand away from the left side of her face.

Lidewij, in particular, had often looked at the calendar, at the picture of the month. They had bought it in Rome, where they had spent a week together just before my arrival, and liked it so much they hung it up early. I have never been close enough to see exactly what they show, those pictures, but I have gathered that they are reproductions of paintings from the Vatican Museum. I remember that months later, in March, I could clearly make out the shape of a cross. I even thought, Why paint a canvas without frame or linen? They certainly came up with some strange subjects, the creators of the past.

But now that it was November, the Vatican calendar referred to days called All Souls' and All Saints'. Lidewij had wondered why, and had suggested that it might be something to do with the leaves of the trees; the last leaves were falling from the trees, and the Vaticanians wanted to celebrate nothing being lost. Her theories made Creator smile.

We're so ignorant about these things, Lidewij said. If you ask me, every day on this calendar means something.

I had already heard him outside, a screech of complaint sounding from the birch wood than ran down to the lake on the left of the deep garden, like a giant cat miaowing a loud lament. I knew he was an animal; I had made that much out from scraps of conversation between Creator and Lidewij. While painting, Creator would imitate his cry, making it sound like *peeow*. After calling, the creature generally walked into the garden to eat chicken feed from an aluminium dish that had been put down just in front of the sliding doors. It was a sound I had often heard while leaning against my wall: something pointy and hard scraping a metal bowl.

Good morning, Creator would say.

It all sounded thoroughly aristocratic. They called him Lord Peacock—but I couldn't imagine what he looked like. According to Lidewij, he had escaped from the playground at Old Valkeveen the previous spring: he heard the pheasants calling during the mating season, and disappeared into the woods. Odd, because pheasants, as I had learnt in the meantime, sound like the horns of old cars, and nowhere near as lofty and elegiac as Lord Peacock.

This is all quite apart from the story of my life, and it has absolutely nothing to do with the fire I am about to feed. But when I finally saw him, that first Saturday in November, when I was free to look out into the world, I felt an immediate pang of regret.

He was as white as a sheet.

He was a completely white creature. As white as me. He was Quadruple-Universal-Primed-Linen white, and yet he could walk. He appeared entirely under his own steam and would, after eating the contents of the bowl, move off somewhere else.

And he didn't notice me.

He scraped the bowl with his vicious beak and dragged a clawed toe towards himself every now and then, making an unpleasant scratching sound. When the chicken feed was finished, he pushed the dish away with an impatient neck movement and looked up.

That was when it happened.

He started to shiver or, better, to shudder, and made gagging movements with his neck and, before I knew it, he had spread his tail, taking up my entire field of vision with his raised, white tail feathers. He didn't stop shuddering; it sounded like he was raising a stormy wind. He made himself even bigger than he was by standing on his toes. The strange thing was that, after the first shock, I immediately realised that it didn't have anything to do with me, this display. He hadn't noticed me at all. He did it because he was seen. But the one who saw him was invisible. *He was impressing* an invisible viewer. I couldn't see it any other way. The garden was deserted, Creator and Lidewij had walked into the woods, and everything in the studio was motionless.

And, despite his improbable whiteness, I saw that his tail feathers, which spread into circles at the ends, meant something; they *were* something. How can I put it? They looked like white circles, but they represented something. I could see that very clearly in the sunlight that lit them from the side; the sun must have been over the birch wood. Yes, what I saw very clearly was that they were eyes — hundreds of white eyes on long, shuddering feathers. Lord Peacock had put up all his eyes to exchange all those glances with someone who was nowhere in sight. And he folded them back down into a much-too-heavy tail that dragged along behind him as he dawdled off in the direction of the wood.

When they came back, Creator lifted me off the easel. I realised to my inexpressible relief that I would not become Cindy. And I ended up back in my corner.

She became a ninety by seventy. Creator mumbled something along the lines of *I paint her mask but capture her soul.* But that was so much bravado because, ultimately, he would remain dissatisfied to the point of fury with the result. Masterful emptiness is what it became — exactly what the art world thought of him. And having Cindy coo with admiration while accepting the painting, smothering Creator with hugs and kisses, telling him he'd done *a hell of a job*, that Fokke would be *ever so moved* and that he, Creator, was a magician who saw right through people and had managed to capture her *ultra-vulnerable self*, didn't make it any better.

Thirty to go and then I'm free.

I actually heard him hum that in those days.

Thirty more portraits.

I realised that he was struggling, fighting for his freedom.

In the meantime, the Cindy has become a famous thing, or so I hear. It even got a reaction from the art world. At least, it seems that, during a radio interview with Minke Dupuis, the curator of the Green Heart Museum said that *Felix Vincent's neo-realist surface was finally acquiring depth.* The curator had seen it hanging in Ponsen's palazzo in Bloemendaal. Minke even managed to elicit the phrase *undertone of tragic emptiness* from the curator.

I mustn't forget to mention that, after coming within a hair's breadth of turning into Cindy, I ended up against the wall in a different position. Not vertical, but horizontal.

It isn't easy to describe what this meant to me. For the first time, it began to dawn on me that I should be prepared for a completely different fate.

December had arrived with an early freeze. Creator kept talking about the reeds at the bottom of the garden, which had taken on a strange rusty colour and stood out superbly against the white of the frozen lake, in which a big hole refused to close over and offered a refuge to dozens of swans that floated on the water as snow-white, dazzling patches. The emptiness, Creator said, the wide, cold emptiness of ice — that's unpaintable.

Emptiness: that was a word he often hummed. He had made a song of it, with, if I understood it properly, a chorus that went, *He dabs and smears them less and less, the canvases of emptiness.*

I smelt the danger immediately.

When Creator says something's unpaintable, he means he's going to paint it.

I really did try to imagine myself as a winter landscape. It wasn't even difficult; I am white by nature, and now that I was horizontal it was easy to think of myself as *wide*. The hole in the ice would come somewhere in my middle, with the ice-cold water and the freezing swans. I couldn't help it—I found it a desolate prospect. I understood very well that, after all these years of painting richer and richer people and, especially after Cindy, a chill had got into Creator's heart. I could see that *something needed to happen to him* if he was to regain his old, inventive zest—but spending the rest of my existence as the embodiment of his disillusionment about Cindy ...

One morning, he set up the easel right in front of the French windows. Then he laid me, lying as I was, across the easel. I stuck out a ridiculous distance on both sides. Somehow I could smell that it was boredom motivating him. Restlessness. He was working on the three children of the charismatic hypnotherapist, Henry Grinke: a girl of ten, boys of six and eight, small format, destined to hang in the cabin cruiser moored in Volendam.

Still, all indications were that this would be the great moment. That I was on the verge of being painted.

I didn't know then that, when Creator really begins, he first applies the *imprimatura* to the canvas. That's an even layer of grey, or drab green, or muddy umber that will determine the tone of the thing. Everything that is added afterwards is conceived from that imprimatura, more or less the way a piece of music is conceived from a melody.

Creator hardly looked at me. He kept his eyes fixed almost constantly on the view behind my back; it was as if the icy surface was reflected in the blue of his eyes, so that they were no longer blue, but metallic grey. I was shocked by the dull emptiness in his eyes and afraid of the thing I would become. If he succeeded in making me look as wintry as his present expression, what kind of chill would pierce the hearts of the people who looked at me when I was finished?

Who would want me?

He was holding a piece of charcoal. I saw now for the first time that he was left-handed.

Suddenly, with an unexpected, angry movement, he drew a horizontal line across me from left to right, from my perspective.

This was his first direct contact with me. The gritty tip of a thin piece of charcoal, which, despite Creator's intention of drawing a line of two metres across the full width of my completely untouched skin, broke off furiously — approximately twenty centimetres before my middle.

Creator swore and kicked the legs of the easel. It fell over, which is to say: we fell over. For a moment, I touched the ground with my left lower corner, then the easel wobbled and tipped forward, with me sliding off it.

I don't know how long Creator left us lying there like that.

Lidewij came in, saying that she had heard a bang. What happened?

Creator wouldn't stop swearing.

You have to get away a bit, Lidewij said. It can't go on like this.

TWO

I was back in my corner when, on the fourth of January that same winter, everything changed. The Vatican calendar, I had heard Lidewij say, showed an Adoration of the Magi. Creator had not cleaned away the charcoal line that ended twenty centimetres before my middle. I felt disfigured, like a man who has had a brand pressed to his forehead by a torturer. And, to add insult to injury, Creator had put me with my back to the wall. For the first time in my life, I felt naked. This then, this state of vulnerability, this inability to protect myself from the eyes of others, was what people call shame.

He arrived in a four-wheel drive. Suddenly, it was as if our woods were full of rhinos, Lidewij would later say. During that first discussion with Creator, which was over in less than thirty minutes, it seems that two young men with alert expressions stayed in the vehicle. Lidewij explained that she had invited them in, but they preferred to wait where they were. One of them was swarthy and very young. North African, Lidewij guessed. They were both clean-shaven and baldheaded.

They made calls now and then on their mobile phones, and once one of them leant against the front of the car to smoke a cigarette. Geese were flying over at the time; that was why Lidewij had stepped out of the kitchen door.

Ah, she thought, geese. The same ones as last year.

That's the kind of thing she tells Creator; she remembers insignificant details. It was exactly one year ago that her mother had been admitted to hospital, and a day later she got the call asking her to come in straightaway because her condition had suddenly deteriorated. Then, too, she had heard long rows of geese over Withernot.

The appointment with the visitor had been made shortly after the failed landscape, about a week after the appearance of the major article in *Palazzo*, in which Creator had said that art needed likeness. If it's not from life, it's from nothing, the headline announced. By-line: Minke Dupuis.

I'd noticed that Creator closed the *Palazzo* the moment he saw the picture of himself with Lidewij in the garden behind Withernot. Rather than being proud, he seemed uncomfortable and didn't deign to look at the text, as if it might be somehow embarrassing.

He doesn't want to look at himself the way he looks at the people who sit for him, I thought later. He is afraid of his own gaze.

In expectation of the visitor, Creator had turned all the paintings he was working on around to face the wall. He always did that before discussions he expected to lead to a commission. He turned around the thing of Beatrix, too, which he had started several days before, commissioned by the Queen's cabinet. For the first time in ten years, a new official portrait was required, and Creator was part of the select group competing for the job, even if he didn't end up getting it. He never managed to turn it into a real Vincent. I can't do a portrait of a stamp, he said, with all the nonchalance he could muster.

The only one Creator didn't turn around was me, with the charcoal line.

The visitor came in, leaning on a stick with an ivory knob, and had difficulty walking. He sat down at the head of the kitchen table that served as a drawing table. During the conversation, he regularly reached for his stick and then held onto it, with his left arm stretched out.

He was skinny. His suit hung loose on his body.

He must have introduced himself upon arriving, in the casual way that powerful people have of introducing themselves. Days would pass before I heard the name, but I didn't need to know that he was called Specht — Valery Specht — and that he was the feared art collector in person, to realise that the studio was alive with a special tension from the moment he entered.

Specht didn't ask Creator to turn any of his things around during that first conversation.

I know the work of Felix Vincent well enough to know why I am here, he said.

Creator did not find it unpleasant to have Specht talk about him in the third person like that; it sounded as if he could just as well have said 'David Hockney' or 'Francis Bacon'.

Felix Vincent, said Specht, is the only one who comes into consideration.

From where I was lying, I had a good view of Specht. And he saw me immediately; I know for a fact that I was the first thing his luminous eagle's eye settled on when he came in. I wished the ground could open up and swallow me. It was as if, for a fraction of a second, he was considering the charcoal line, as if to decide whether I was art. Interesting. Buyable. Then he turned back to Creator. His piercing gaze smouldered on, in the spot where the smudge of charcoal ended, exactly twenty centimetres before my middle.

The whites of his eyes were not white, but yellow. Intriguing piece, he said, in *Palazzo*.

Yes, Creator said.

I saw it last week and I thought, Felix Vincent, he's someone I'd like to meet.

His voice was rasping and high, as if it had never

broken, with an unmistakable Rotterdam accent. I noticed that, like me, Creator was fascinated by his long bony hands, his thin wrists, and the emaciated face above the alarmingly long, Adam's apple-less neck. He had a brush of short grey hair, the ash-grey of someone who was once blond.

Did it work out, the Pietà?

I heard Creator's breath catch.

How do you —?

His eyes went to the *Palazzo* lying on the table, and he realised that Minke Dupuis had not kept to their agreement.

When I read that, Specht said, that you wanted to start on that, with a theme like that, I knew. You, I can ask. He's got balls.

Creator remembered Specht's bright gaze as the gaze of a painter.

He looked at things like someone who creates, he said to Lidewij afterwards.

Still, this first introductory phase was no test of strength. Specht had sounded too sad for that. Tired and sad. He looked around the room again.

Ah, he said. There's Jeanine.

He stood up and walked over to the wall she was hanging on.

You know her?

Someone once sent her to me, as a postcard.

Funnily, Creator didn't ask whom. He didn't want

to show how overwhelmingly flattered he suddenly felt.

Specht had sat down again.

I actually only have one question, he said.

His voice, which had been very quiet the whole time, had become virtually inaudible.

Do you also work from death?

He didn't wait for Creator's answer. His left hand was clenched around the knob of his stick, but he had slowly slipped his free hand into the inside pocket of his jacket.

I don't think he was expecting an answer.

He had pulled a chequebook out from his inside pocket.

Before I tell you what it's about, I want you to know that I am offering you one hundred thousand. Euros. Fifty thousand now, and fifty thousand on completion.

Specht brought thumb and index finger to his lips, licked them, leafed the chequebook open, and wrote down five figures. He then slid the chequebook to the middle of the table, where Creator could see it with his own eyes. It said €50,000. All it needed was tearing out and signing.

Creator managed to resist touching the cheque.

I know for a fact that he did the internal Withernot calculation and realised: this saves months. Fifteen portraits. Forty-five sessions. The amount was fifteen times his current asking price, even for his most time-consuming thing. *Aunt Drea can die now.*

Creator had not noticed that Specht was observing him closely.

You know better than anyone else that a Vincent is worth it, Specht said. Shall we drop the formality? Call me Valery.

Creator tried as hard as he could to look relaxed. He cannot remember anyone ever looking at him as defiantly as in that moment.

Felix, he said.

Your work is fascinating, Specht continued. You have a rare skill. You can bring someone to life.

Only now did I notice that, despite the calm with which he spoke, Specht was perspiring. There were little beads on his forehead, and a glistening edge just below his hairline.

I realise full well that I am asking you to do something you've never done before, Specht said. Not for a moment did his left hand stop rubbing the knob of his walking stick.

Don't say no straightaway. Think it over. You'll be saving a life.

He was tired, I could see that plainly now. Dead tired. Or deathly ill.

Again his right hand moved towards his inside pocket.

I'm asking you for a portrait. Of my son. He's dead.

Specht had laid a photo next to the chequebook. Creator slid it closer.

Specht, a father! That was as difficult to imagine as a round Mondrian, he would later tell Lidewij. For a moment, I was at a complete loss for words.

As far as Creator knew, Specht, who had inherited a well-known dredging company, had gone through public life in the exclusive company of young men.

Creator concentrated on the photo.

Loutro, Specht said. You know Loutro?

Creator shook his head.

He had been prepared for many things, but not this: a holiday snap showing two blond children, a boy and a girl, with their arms around a slightly smaller, dark-skinned boy. Loutro is Crete, Specht said. South coast. We've got a place there.

He pointed at something in the photo.

That's the corner of our terrace.

Specht looked at Creator.

It's about my son.

With difficulty, Creator looked away from the dark boy with the dark expression, who was in the process of raising his middle finger. He concentrated on the laughing boy on the right, who was making a V sign with his left hand.

Nice-looking kid. First form?

The photo was taken seven years ago, Specht said.

Then your son would have been nineteen now?

Creator was feeling his way as he spoke, trying to find the tone in which to speak about a dead child with a man who was old enough to be his own father.

There was a silence in which Specht seemed to be adding something up, but it wasn't that. He said, It's about Singer. In the middle.

He didn't give Creator time to recover from his surprise. He didn't give him a chance to ask, Is your wife black then? Let alone, Are you married? or, Do you have a wife?

Later, he would tell Lidewij that he had only had one thought in his head: all of the one hundred and fifty portraits that made up his oeuvre at that moment were of white people. He felt uncomfortable, as if entering unknown territory, a minefield of sensitivities.

This photo was taken three years before Singer's death, Specht said.

Creator looked at the dark boy with the half-raised middle finger, who was now irrevocably called Singer and had now irrevocably died four years ago, and he felt like he was twisting into the boy's eyes, like water irrevocably swirling down the plughole of a bath.

Smiling lips, suspicious eyes.

It was so quiet in the studio that I wondered whether Creator actually understood what Specht was going to ask him to do. I had worked it out long since; I felt myself tight with tension from stretcher to stretcher. Creator didn't know a thing about that boy and yet his consciousness was suddenly fully occupied with a single spiralling thought. He told Lidewij about it later. *Everyone I have painted will die. And every painting will one day be seen the way I now look at this snapshot.*

Why is he dead? Creator realised how strange his question sounded.

Do you really want to know?

It was the first time Specht smiled.

Is it necessary to know why someone died? I mean, if you had Singer before you now, alive, and you had agreed to do his portrait, would you want to know how he was going to meet his end?

Creator got the impression that Specht had carefully prepared this part of the conversation.

That sounds like a story by Borges, doesn't it? The portrait artist who knew how his sitters would meet their end …

The silence he left now was commanding.

I have to admit, he said, that I wondered whether to tell whoever gets the job that Singer is dead at all. But you would have asked why he hadn't come with me.

Absolutely, Creator said. I've only ever worked from life.

I know, Specht said. You say so yourself in *Palazzo*: If it's not from life, it's from nothing. And that is exactly what I am about to ask. Paint my son. Bring him to life. Forget he's dead.

I could see that Specht's face had become imploring. The expression I had, up to that moment, taken for the weariness of an invalid now looked like the exhaustion of someone who was completely miserable. A drop of sweat rolled past his temple. But Creator still couldn't bring himself to say that he would accept the job.

Think about it, Specht said. This isn't the only photo I have of Singer; there's a video, too. I can describe him. He pulled the chequebook back towards him, tore off the top cheque, and got the fountain pen back out from his inside pocket.

Believe me, he said, with every word sounding more and more whispered. *You'll be saving a life.*

Creator remained silent. I remember that very well; it was because he was shocked by something he could not place at all, something that was diametrically opposed to the self-assured Hollywood gesture with the cheque: all of the blood in Specht's face seemed to have drained away.

There wasn't a lovelier person on the whole planet, he said.

What I'm asking for, Felix, is Singer. My son.

Specht signed the cheque.

Afterwards, when Creator had shown Valery Specht to the door and returned to the studio, I knew not only that he would accept the job, but also that I was the one who was destined to support Singer.

Or however you say that.

It was on me that the unknown dead boy would be commemorated and painted to life.

Strangely enough, I seemed to know this before Creator himself—at least, the only thing he said to Lidewij a little later, when she came into the studio, was that he had had a request that was completely wacko, a job that nobody in their right mind would ever take on.

But in the meantime he had slid me into the middle of the room and leant me against the easel. He had squatted down and used a small brush to clean off the charcoal line. He did it like a household chore, but I rejoiced within because I was certain that it was a gesture. He had begun to really want me; he just didn't know it yet.

Moments before, he had put the cheque away in the drawer of the large table, between the pencil stubs and the rubbers; but when Lidewij came in to hear how the meeting had gone, he told her everything—except about the cheque.

It just happened: putting away the cheque and sliding me into view. He would keep quiet about the cheque and the amount, and he brushed off the charcoal. None of it was something he'd planned in advance.

I mention this because, later, Creator got the cheque back out of the drawer a few times. I was on the easel by then, and Creator had slipped into his habit of rhyming and calculating. That's how I know with absolute certainty that he was thinking one, compulsive thought, If I take the cheque and cash it, then—

Nothing much followed that *then*, except an ungrammatical construction ending with *trash it*—after which he put the cheque back in its hiding place.

No hurry, he mumbled.

Specht has to see the thing first and accept it.

Lidewij listened carefully to his account of his first meeting with Specht.

Were they really his words, she asked—*If you've ever worked from death?*

She whistled through her teeth.

Creator noticed how difficult it was to explain just

what was so strange about Specht's request.

And then Specht said you'd be saving a life?

Creator nodded.

Imagine, Lidewij said. Your son is dead and you want to be able to see him; you want to have him around you again. What an assignment, Felix. What an assignment.

Creator had told her the little that Specht had said about Singer: that he came from Africa, from one of the countries on the west coast. The name had slipped Creator's mind for a moment; it was synonymous with chaos and cruelty. Specht had spent some time there for a big job, almost under war conditions; it was an enormous dredging job, and on the beach just near the compound he'd stumbled upon a boy of about eight, literally stumbled—the child was asleep on the lawn in front of the apartment block. It was in the days when rural children were being press-ganged into a rebel army in the north. Imagine it, a boy like that asleep on the lawn—he opens his eyes and wants to trust you; imagine the coincidence. But what is coincidence in moments like this other than providence? Singer was looking for *him*, Specht. Specht wasn't looking for Singer. Anyway, in the end, it was all done completely legally, with all the adoption papers fully in order—you can't imagine the red tape involved—and, of course, as always in those parts, it took a lot of ... not just money, but also, let's call it diplomatic pressure that didn't come cheap. For him, it had been nothing short of a miracle that it finally succeeded.

Did he mention anyone else?

What do you mean?

It usually takes two to adopt.

There was something, Creator said.

Has she got a name?

If she's a she, Creator said. All I know is they live in Antibes. Specht and —

She? Did he say *she*?

Does it matter?

If you ask me, they both wanted to say that it mattered whether Specht was married to a man or a woman, but they just laughed it off.

No, Lidewij said. For the painting, it doesn't matter. Or does it?

She didn't ask whether Creator had accepted the job. But she did look at the photo lying on the big table.

Crete, Creator said.

Lidewij looked at the photo and fell silent.

Her gaze was drawn into the boy's eyes, just like Creator's a half hour earlier, in Specht's presence.

Hey, kid, she said quietly. Where are you?

She had sounded as if the boy in the photo was still alive. As if the photo was a living person and could answer her.

I think that was the moment that Creator knew what I already knew: that he would paint Singer.

Lidewij passed the photo back to Creator.

Did you see his hand? The one he's giving the finger with. He doesn't have a thumb.

Creator looked again at the boy called Singer.

Now you mention it, he said.

It's incredible how people can just disappear, Lidewij said. Did you hear the geese over the house just now? Hundreds of them?

I am certain that Creator then thought, *I'll paint him.*

Look at Lidewij, I thought. Look at your wife, at how the photo has just touched her, and make something that touches her just as much. And Specht. And everyone who has lost someone. Make something. Make someone. From me.

THREE

Creator decided to stick as closely as possible to the working methods he used when painting someone who was alive. In other words, he arranged three sittings with Specht. During these fortnightly Saturday meetings, each of which lasted for several hours, they would talk about Singer, leaf through albums of snapshots, and watch the videos that had been made of him. In the meantime, Creator did sketches to show Specht; but he soon realised that, just as when he was working from life, the likeness would not be the problem.

The problem was the expression or, rather, the movement in his eyes — the characteristic gesture. Technically, Singer was a challenge mainly because of the colour of his skin. New tints would appear on Creator's palette: dioxide purple, carmine, ultramarine, burnt umber, caput mortuum, cadmium yellow. Creator explained to Specht that, when he was working on a thing, the skin was the alpha and the omega. You don't look at my things with just your eyes, he had said to Minke Dupuis in *Palazzo*; you use your fingertips as well.

He would soon decide to base the portrait on one particular video recording, the one that had been shot early in the morning, or was it late in the evening, where the camera enters a room in which a dark, underexposed figure — Singer — is lying asleep on a large bed with green, almost turquoise, sheets, with his knuckles to his mouth, and his head turned aside towards the window whose venetian blinds are slowly opened during the shot, making a pattern of bright stripes of light that are about to make the motionless, sleeping figure blink. That is the precise moment at which the recording stops, just when the eye contact with the camera is about to be established.

It wasn't easy to estimate Singer's age in the video. He was naked and, as Creator saw it, more angular than in the photo with his blond friends. If he was sixteen in the video, Creator asked Specht, how long before that was the photo taken? Specht's memory didn't seem very precise with things like this. Creator realised that he would have to decide for himself how old Singer would be in his painting.

The green of the sheets was pushing it, Creator said, but everything of value balances on the edge of kitsch. He wanted the pink of Singer's lips and nails and the palms of his hands to burst out of the painting. He was searching for a Singer who was more childlike, less remote, than in the video.

When Creator saw the video recording, he knew

immediately that Singer would be lying down — and I resigned myself to my fate. I was *horizontal* now to stay, but didn't really care, almost blinded as I was by the concentration in Creator's eyes when he came to stand before me now and then, without touching me with a single finger. By that time, he had studied Singer at length, projected larger than life on a white wall. He continually skipped forward a few images, for hours at a time, as if each jump might provide the one glimpse of Singer that would definitively put him to work. And then he tore himself away from the projection and looked at me with a sated expression, as if trying to project what he had seen onto me. Once he even aimed the video projector at me, which had an alarming effect, not just because of the intense heat of the light, but also because I felt like I was moving, even though Singer himself was only sleeping on me. It was a foolish experiment; Creator concluded that soon enough, but it made me realise that I could count myself very lucky not to have come into the world as a film screen. I couldn't do it — exist inasmuch as light moved over me. You'd have to be some kind of saint for that.

It was a sun-drenched scene, the one Creator was basing the portrait on. When the video was playing, you heard children's voices through the open window behind the venetians. That was Loutro beach, Specht said; the ship's horn you can hear is the ferry to Chora

Sfakion. It moored three times a day right in front of our house.

Paradise, Creator said, and Specht gave a vague smile.

Creator tried to ask how long exactly before Singer's death the video had been made.

Sometimes Creator got the impression that the sight of the dead boy was too much for Specht to bear: beads of sweat would start running down his temples again, and his white-knuckled hand would clench his stick.

Creator pointed at Singer's upper arms, his visible shoulder, and his thigh — there was something glittering there, beach sand, streaks of white gold.

Yes, I see it now, too, Specht said. I never noticed it.

Skin, Creator said. A painting is actually just a skin applied to a skin.

It was clear that Specht was doing his utmost to make Creator forget that his subject was dead, and Creator got better and better at playing along. They soon stopped talking about the boy in the past tense.

That is the grand purpose of our enterprise, Specht said. If I succeed in making Singer live for you, it will be as if you have painted him from life. Then how could he be dead?

You see, he said on another occasion, if you succeed in making people believe you painted from life, then I have succeeded in making him live for you.

He also said, This way, no one's dead.

There was no mention of the circumstances in which Singer had died. The less you think of his end, the more alive it will be. As alive as a Felix Vincent, Specht said.

The only thing he told Creator was that it was an accident.

A stupid accident.

On Crete?

The movement of Specht's left hand over the knob of his walking stick was a clear indication that Creator should not pursue this line of questioning.

On another occasion, he asked whether Singer had been born without a thumb.

You don't miss a thing, do you?

Here, too, Specht refused to be drawn. Creator got the impression that he knew very little about Singer's life before he was eight, when he moved from Sierra Leone to Antibes. When he was taken there. Singer spoke a bit of French by then, African French, and must have spoken the language of the tribe he came from, but Specht was never, so he said, able to find out which tribe that was. And in the South of France, Singer's French became more and more French.

Creator asked about Singer's voice.

While sketching, he had become increasingly aware of how important the voice of the person he was painting was to him under normal circumstances. He couldn't say just what difference it made to the painting itself, but it was somehow key to his concentration. More than anything else, the voice played a major role when he was working on a painting after the sitter had returned home. It was then that he really heard the accent—whether it was loud or quiet, the way the speaker interrupted their own sentences and paused. As if painting was Creator's way of carrying out an imaginary conversation with someone.

Specht asked whether he had played with dolls when he was a child.

That might explain it, Creator chuckled in reply. Maybe that was when I learnt it, doing portraits. And he told Specht that he had been an only child and, for as far back as he could remember, had drawn one special face, very crude, but that was Tulix. That was what he called the face, and he used to talk to it, until he was eight or nine at least.

No, Specht said during that same conversation, we don't know whether Singer had a brother or a sister. I wonder if he ever really was a child at play in his whole life.

One day, Creator also told Specht about the blind woman he once painted, at her husband's request. At the end of the story, which didn't really have a point, other than that Creator had to keep the conversation going throughout the sitting to keep the woman from turning away from him, Specht asked, Why are you telling me this?

Because it ended up as one of my worst things, even more dismal than Cindy. That's one of the reasons this, this thing of Singer, is so difficult now. Because he doesn't look back. Do you understand? I'm starting to see him before me. I think I know exactly how I'm going to arrange him as well, how I'm going to put him on the canvas, but …

Creator hesitated, I believe because he now realised what was so difficult about the commission.

The blind woman had no idea, he told Specht. Do you understand? She didn't realise I was searching for something, she wasn't trying to hide anything, she couldn't see how I was looking at her — and that's why I, in turn, didn't actually see anything. Nothing particularly paintable, I mean.

Specht nodded seriously.

You'll find something, he said. Really, I am absolutely convinced of that. Suddenly you'll have it, and Singer will become your masterpiece. All the things that make it difficult will make it different from everything you've done up to now.

Specht was silent for a few seconds while Creator advanced the video. I didn't have a good view of Specht, but I heard him give a whispered cry, between a sigh and a groan. Creator must have heard it, too. It was as if he moaned, *Mercy* or, *Spare me.* They weren't really words you could make out. Creator was moved. Later, he told Lidewij that he now knew that pictures could be fatal.

He broke out into a cold sweat, he said. I thought his heart was breaking.

He's not playing around, Lidewij said. This is deadly serious. But it will be the most beautiful thing you've ever done.

My masterpiece, according to Specht. He knows how to butter me up.

Those were the kind of things they were saying even before the imprimatura had been applied.

Creator added, after a long silence, that it was only now that he understood why he had become a painter. And he told Lidewij that the thing would be horizontal, with Singer as an awakening sleeper, head to toe.

So it'll be a nude, Lidewij said.

Creator didn't answer — because this, as I now realised, was the question.

Lidewij never got to see the video of Singer motionless—I didn't, either, at that stage. They were ridiculously strict about things like that, Creator and Lidewij. Even before entering his studio for the very first time, she had told him that she never wanted to see any of his work that wasn't finished. Not a sketch, not a scribble, nothing. If I get drawn into the process of thinking about what you're making, there'll be no end to it. I have enough on my plate with who you are. She kept to this resolution with ritual determination. She can enter Creator's studio and stop in front of the thing he's working on without noticing anything about the painting at all. And Creator knows it: he has got completely out of the habit of thinking that she, when standing there, sees anything of his work. It is only when a painting has been completed, and it's time for the client to come and pick it up, that Creator asks Lidewij *to finish the thing off.* That's what he calls it. For him, her first look at what he has made is as decisive as his own signature—which he generally adds immediately afterwards.

So it'll be a nude.

Creator understood the ramifications of Lidewij's

suggestion perfectly. Singer, nude — it was almost inevitable, and yet it had to be decided. During his sittings with Specht, Creator had realised more and more clearly that the only correct name for the expression he always sought, the one that got him started on each new portrait, was the *naked expression*. Specht had said as much as well, in the beginning, before asking him to call him Valery. I admire the shyness of your work. Gesturing at Jeanine.

If, with Singer, it was not possible to find that expression — that special, shy vulnerability — then surely his entire self needed to be naked.

Specht didn't interrupt while Creator proposed it during the last sitting. He described the enormity of it: two metres wide, one metre twenty high, a sea of sea-green sheets and pillows, the angled light of evening falling through an invisible window on the right ... and Specht smiled.

This was what he had secretly hoped for, he said. Something more than a portrait, but he hadn't wanted to suggest it himself.

A twelve-year-old nude?

Creator nodded.

That will take courage, Specht said. A twelve-year-old nude.

Creator gave him a questioning look.

Nothing is as difficult as innocence, Specht said. Or as rare. Nothing as scandalous, either.

It seemed to me, at that moment, as if Creator was overcome by a strange sensation of Specht and Lidewij conspiring together to put him to work — their reactions to his intentions, although entirely independent of each other, seemed motivated by such similar thinking. Sometimes he even felt as if the commission wasn't just coming from Specht, but from Lidewij, too. As if it wasn't just about Singer, who had really existed and could be seen on videos and photographs, but also about someone who did *not yet* exist.

He'll be on a green background, Creator said at one stage. A sea of folds.

A sea, Specht said. He got used to the idea.

Or do you mean a womb?

Creator realised that, for the first time in his life, he, the photographic realist, was going to do something fundamentally different from working from life. Instead of capturing something that he had seen, as if in a flash, he had to start on someone who was fundamentally elsewhere.

Creator didn't put it like that, of course. Words like *fundamentally elsewhere* never passed his lips. He described the unknown territory Singer would take him into by saying that if he didn't pull it off, *his arse would be showing.*

A womb, that's the word, Creator said. A womb of sea-green folds.

When Specht said goodbye after the third session, Creator was, if I'm not mistaken, almost as feverish as when he came to pick me up from Van Schendel's. Before saying goodbye, Specht had asked, unnecessarily, So I take it you really have accepted this commission?

Creator, equally unnecessarily, assented.

They were again sitting at the large table.

All I can do now is wish you strength, Specht said.

Specht stuck a hand in his inside pocket and left it dangling there awkwardly for a long time, as if making a tremendously difficult decision.

Perhaps this will be of some use to you, he said, pulling out a Polaroid.

His long, bony hand trembled and flapped as if he had lost control of his muscles. He let go of his stick to help his right hand with his left. The stick fell clattering to the floor. Creator leapt forward to pick it up.

For a moment, the studio was full of fluttering consternation, as if a gust of wind had torn through it.

When Creator sat down again, the Polaroid was in front of him. Specht watched closely, studying his expression.

Creator could not suppress a sigh of disappointment. For a moment, he had hoped to finally catch Singer's eye. But the Polaroid revealed little more than the video. The same bed, the same pose: Singer with his eyes shut. The only difference was that the fold of sheet that covered Singer's genitals on the video had now been slid a few inches to the left, but without making Singer fundamentally any more naked—Creator saw that immediately.

Thanks, he said. Every little bit helps.

Specht cleared his throat. Clearly, he found it difficult to speak.

When will my son be ready?

Without thinking, Creator said, Easter.

Easter was a couple of months away. He seldom allowed so much time.

Specht seemed fully recovered. He looked at his watch, and asked whether it would be all right for him to pick Singer up on Holy Saturday.

Creator glanced at the calendar. Is that what it's called? Holy Saturday?

One last thing, Specht said, after making the appointment. In no way must it get out that you have accepted this commission. Or that I have given it.

Creator replied that he had already said that that went without saying during their first meeting. That wasn't true at all; he had never said anything of the kind. Much later, he would tell Lidewij that he couldn't understand why he had been in such a hurry to let Specht know that he understood that the commission was top secret.

Not a soul gets to see Singer, you understand?

At that moment, Lidewij appeared outside carrying skates, headed for the ice at the end of the garden. She waved briefly to Creator and Specht.

Except Lidewij, Creator said.

If there's no way round it, Specht said. But otherwise, not a soul. And the material — the videos, the photos — no one gets access to it. And no one takes any photos of him when he's finished. Not one.

He had started sounding like the captain of industry he had not been at all in the last few weeks, emaciated and diseased as he was.

No photo, no Polaroid, nothing.

Creator didn't know whether to laugh or be angry, he told Lidewij afterwards. It was actually rather pathetic, that last moment before Specht's departure, when he reached for his mobile phone to let his chauffeur and the smoking dark-skinned youth, who were waiting at the four-wheel drive just a few dozen metres away, know that he was on his way.

The way he was going, Creator said, I wouldn't have been surprised if he'd said, If anyone sees Singer, I will turn you into a tube of paint.

After the car had driven out of the garden and disappeared into the woods, Creator realised they hadn't said another word about the money.

I saw him walk to the drawer to check whether

the cheque was still there. He stood in the studio's winter light and listened until the sound of Specht's car dissolved in the woods around Withernot. He kept his eyes fixed on me the whole time — but I don't think he saw me.

I didn't really understand what it means to be a support until the imprimatura had been applied. Something appears on you, but you don't get to see it. That's what it comes down to. You see the looks of others taking in more and more, but understand less and less about yourself. Of course, being painted is an indescribable experience: first with the wide, flat brush with which the imprimatura is applied — in this particular case, raw umber — and then, several drying days later, with the pointed, lightning-fast brush that draws the outline of the depiction on you, with sketching, self-correcting movements; and finally, for many weeks, with countless brushes of constantly varying thickness and pointedness, slowly but surely concealing what you have been up to this point — the canvas. But no matter how unguent and stimulating the period of creation is, it all goes to impress upon you ever more harrowingly that you can only become the great unknown of your own existence.

Now that I really think about it, I found it a period of mindlessness more than anything else, regardless of how sensual and sensational the paint drying on my skin sometimes felt. Creator was continuously humming, mumbling, drinking coffee, taking a few steps back, biting his lips, hissing through his teeth, sticking the little finger of his right hand up his nose, studying what he had picked out of it, looking at me again, squeezing the end of a tube flat, walking over to the window, strolling to the table, studying the Polaroid, striding back over to me, squinting, adding a brushstroke ... He was, to me, at his least savoury. I had the strong impression that he thought himself completely unwatched, as it were; he was all eyes, looking not just at what he was making but also, and mostly, at nothing. I have no better word for it — it seemed to me that very often he was staring at nothing, with an empty, if not dead, look, staring at the garden, where it had started to thaw, at the cuticle of his thumb, at a detail on me that was apparently finished.

Lidewij wasn't around — she had gone skiing for a couple of weeks with a friend — so I couldn't expect any relief from her. This was besides the fact that she, when standing opposite me before I was finished, would have no doubt limited herself to resolutely non-seeing glances. And I had a strong suspicion that Creator's feverish compulsion to work was also related to Lidewij's absence. He was the kind of person who wasn't good at being alone in a house that was completely empty; but when he found himself in that situation, it released forces within him, a voracious restlessness that didn't know when to stop.

It wasn't until Creator reached a spot in the middle, about twenty centimetres more or less to the left of my middle, that I picked up some kind of creative tension from him. I mean, it was only then that he was like the creator I had imagined and only then that I saw that painting really was difficult and demanding. He painted for a quarter of an hour with the squinting concentration of a bomb-disposal expert. All things considered, this was the only moment in which I thought I was going to be something special.

One day I was finished.

That, at least, was my conclusion from the way Creator came into the studio without choosing a brush, without picking up the triangular piece of particle board he used as a palette, without squeezing out a tube of paint. He just came over to stand before me and looked.

Holy moly, he said.

Beyond expectations, he said as well and, Calling all nations. And, Boy-oh-boy, he knows his stuff.

He took a step towards me and bent forward, towards the spot in my middle, and started humming.

Nothing wrong with that, he mumbled to himself.

I felt like he wasn't looking at his own work, but at something new that just happened to have been placed in his studio.

Good job, he said out loud. A bloody good job.

He took a large step to the side and bent forward again. This was where Singer's face was. I knew that, because I had sometimes heard Creator swearing, just there, because it was so bloody difficult, a flat nose like that. He didn't want it turning into *Tintin in the Congo*.

He looked at the wind-up alarm clock that stood on a crate somewhere in the studio. It was four o'clock in the afternoon. I heard the car keys tinkling in his left hand. Only now did I notice that he was wearing different clothes—only his shoes showed that he was a painter.

Suddenly he spoke directly to me, speaking loudly and clearly. What do you reckon? You ready?

I understood what he meant.

Am I finished?

It was, I can't put it any other way, a moment of splitting. Not for Creator—but for me. He had spoken directly to me before, with a question he already knew the answer to. But this time it was as if the question was no longer for me, but for someone else—the person who had ended up on me. It was for Singer, who I had to assume was the person who was now on me. I realise how hopeless my sentences are becoming; my grammar is not up to my history. When Creator spoke to me he was no longer speaking to me, but to Singer. But who was I if I was Singer?

Oh, van Schendel, who was I if I was Singer?

Brace yourself, Creator said. Lidewij will zoom down out of the sky and then she'll see you, hie-dee-hie.

He winked.

I had rarely seen him so childish or carefree.

Good luck, he said and disappeared, rattling the car keys.

Without Lidewij, Withernot had been dead quiet. Singer had arisen in silence, underground, as it were. For weeks, Creator hadn't seen or spoken to anyone; he hadn't answered the phone or known another person's glance.

It was as if I had become something terrible — I can't put it any other way.

I don't know how I came to this idea, because the last glance Creator gave me before driving to Schiphol to pick up Lidewij was cheerful. Elated. And yet, during the ninety minutes that separated me from Lidewij's return, I felt like someone who is regaining consciousness after a coma and is about to see for the first time how others react to his burnt, disfigured face. Don't ask me how I came to this horrific thought — what did I know of disfigurement, I, who from the far corner of my left eye had only very rarely seen the movement on the television in the adjoining room?

I only knew about disasters and blazing infernos inasmuch as they were discussed on the evening news and current affairs programmes. I was shocked by the intensity with which I suddenly knew that my face was burnt — it was as if I had a memory that wasn't mine.

Creator wasn't there when Lidewij stepped into the sunroom. It was getting on for six. He had taken her skis to the shed before lugging her suitcase upstairs to the washing machine. He obviously wanted to give her some time alone with me first.

Strangely enough, she didn't walk up to me after coming into the room. Instead she strode over to the far-left corner to tug on the cord of the venetian blinds, which were hanging down at an angle in front of the section of window that was furthest from me.

The day had been overcast, but a wind had risen in the course of the afternoon and long March clouds were racing across the sky. There seemed to be as many clouds as patches of blue.

In the very moment the blinds uncovered the window, a cloud moved away from the sun and an almost horizontal beam of light shone into the studio. It seemed to skim in just over my right-hand corner; for a second, I understood what it must be like to screw your eyes up against a glare.

Lidewij turned and smiled.

Rather than looking at me, she was looking, as far as I could tell, along the beam of light that shone into the sunroom and lit up the side wall to my right or diagonally above me.

The light was coming from behind her. I saw her as a black patch with overexposed edges.

She stayed standing there like that while the sun sank into the tops of the birches bordering that part of the garden. It took less than a minute. Only then did she come up to me and turn into Lidewij. Tanned, blond, skiing-holiday Lidewij, with her apple-green scarf and her red lips — she was the first person to see me. At that moment, and I am fairly sure of this, I was not thinking of Creator's promise to Specht not to show me to anyone, that *not a soul on earth gets to see Singer.*

Lidewij stood there and looked at me or, rather, she looked at the person who had arisen on me over the last few weeks, and that person, finally seen, opened his eyes — that's what it felt like to me — and saw her.

Immediately after the imprimatura, when Creator sketched Singer's outline on me, I realised more or less where my face would be. And later, when he spent hours working on two closely adjacent spots in that same area with a tickling, unspeakably fine brush, I knew that that was where my eyes must be — but what did I know? Whether they were closed, drooping, or wide open — I had no idea. But now, now that Lidewij, after a flashing glance which seemed to take me in as a whole, let her own eyes be drawn to the place where I knew my eyes to be, I became, or liked to think of myself as having become, really seen for the first time.

Strange, how soon this exchange of looks was over.

Had I expected her to gaze into my eyes for minutes at a time like a lover or a young mother communing with her child?

I had absolutely no sense of something having been exchanged.

I noticed to my dismay that there was no question at all of eyes seeking eyes.

This confused me so much that the gesture that followed took me completely by surprise.

In the unfathomably brief span of time after the incomprehensible exchange of looks, her gaze had slid to the left, away from my face, to the spot twenty centimetres left of centre—where Creator had spent the last two days before Lidewij's return working with the same concentration and intensity he had brought to my eyes. And before I knew what was happening, Lidewij had stepped forward and touched me.

There.

Involuntarily, like someone touching the fontanel of a newborn.

She said that a few minutes later, when Creator came into the studio. She used the word fontanel, which I heard for the first time in my life. Creator smiled when he heard her say that word, and I noticed his right hand slide briefly, involuntarily, towards his crotch.

I didn't feel it. I mean: Lidewij had already touched me and pulled her hand back again before I realised what was happening. She looked, apparently shocked, at the tips of her index and middle fingers, but there was no paint on them.

She stepped back and sighed.

Then she used the fingertips that had touched me to wipe the corner of her right eye.

Felix?

She hadn't taken her eyes off me, but Creator had already entered the studio and was standing behind her, looking with her.

Felix, come here! Look at this.

Mysterious words. She knew he had painted me.

But still she said, Felix, come here! — as if wanting to show me to him.

Look at this.

She turned and laid her head on his chest, as if to hear the beating of his heart.

It was getting dark.

I saw Creator looking at me over her head, as if trying to see me through her eyes.

Who is he, Felix?

That is what she asked. And when no answer came, she asked again in different words.

Who were you thinking of, Felix, when you painted him?

Creator pulled away from her and mumbled, No one.

She grabbed his head with both hands. He answered the gesture by pulling her shoulders towards him.

I missed you, Lidewij said. Come on, okay?

Without another word, they disappeared to the right, out of the studio. I heard their feet drumming up the stairs. Above me, the washing machine was already on. I heard them in the bedroom, too, kicking off their shoes.

It had been a tear—that was what she, Lidewij, had wiped away with her fingertips—I was sure of it.

Who were you thinking of, Felix, when you painted him?

That was what she had asked, and when they came back into the studio a half-hour later—her in her red dressing-gown and apple-green sneakers, him with his T-shirt hanging out of his jeans and socks on his feet—she asked it again.

Creator realised that this time Lidewij would not be fobbed off with mumbles. He loved her, I think, because she was able to ask him questions he had to answer, even if he didn't know how.

Does it matter?

You must have been thinking of someone special, she said. Not just Singer. You must have been.

It's a strange question, he said. Is that what you'd ask the father of a newborn?

Yes, she said. That's exactly what I'd ask. If you ask me, it's an awfully good question. Who do you think of when you make a baby?

She had wrapped an arm around his waist, and his arm was draped over her shoulder. She closed her eyes to let him kiss her eyelids one after the other. Creator knew what her answer would be, but he still asked the question.

Who were you thinking of? Just then, upstairs?

Mum, she said. If I was thinking of anyone — just then, upstairs — it was at least partly Mum.

She was silent for a moment, then looked at me. My face, I mean.

And him, she said. I kept seeing Singer.

Upstairs, the washing machine started to spin, sending a shiver through the house.

She knew that for now she wouldn't be getting any more of an answer out of Creator, nothing more than an embrace. And to tell the truth, I don't really know whether it's an important part of my story who was on his mind while he was working on me. I mean, what difference would it make if we found out that, while painting the *Mona Lisa*, Leonardo da Vinci was constantly thinking of Gladys Grady?

But Creator still wanted to answer. And later—when Lidewij was overdue and had even bought a pregnancy test, which she then made a point of not using as she, as she put it, had already known for ages that it had caught, caught with a vengeance—Felix, there isn't a colour in the world that could indicate something like that—Creator told her about Tijn.

Lidewij had just asked him whether she shouldn't take the Polaroid. Of me. Traditionally, that was her job. When a picture was ready and she had *finished the thing off* by being the first to look at it, she would take a photo for the records.

No need, Creator said. I've already done it.

That was true, and it had been a peculiar moment—Creator gazing through a camera at me in order to transfer me to another support. Because that, at least, I had figured out. This was a device for moving the portrait I had become somewhere else—every last bit of it, but *in another format*. It worked by flash, an instantaneous explosion of light that came out of the device and made me feel as if I had been turned invisible, swallowed up entirely by brightness. For that one instant, I thought, Now I am a blank canvas again.

That wasn't the case. A small support came sliding out of the camera, and a minute or two later, with Creator rubbing it on his right sleeve, I appeared on it. Not that I got to see myself. I deduced that I was there on the Polaroid from the way Creator looked from one to the other, from the Polaroid to me, and back again, comparing what he saw. He seemed satisfied with the result. Creator put the Polaroid away in the drawer in the large table, the one containing the cheque and his pencil stubs. A strange, nagging emptiness is what I had felt, as if the photo had been taken *from* me rather than *of* me.

I certainly had no sensation of being doubled or reborn. To be honest, I forgot the Polaroid soon enough, but later the Vatican calendar showed a painting of something called a shroud. The word meant nothing to me, but from Lidewij's conversation I deduced that long ago someone had pressed a cloth against the face of an unforgettable man who was either dying or had just died. Centuries later, people discovered that an imprint of his face was still visible on the cloth. It was as if the dead man existed again. Or had never stopped existing. I noticed that Lidewij's thoughts had turned to her mother and I was right, because a little later she said that she kept the last glass her mother had drunk out of in a cabinet and had never washed it. Her lips left a print on it, she said, and that's why that glass is Mum.

In a manner of speaking, Creator said.

No, Lidewij said, strangely passionate. Not at all in a manner of speaking. The glass is even more Mum's mouth now than when her mouth existed.

They were sitting in garden chairs pushed up against the sunroom wall on the right, positioned to catch the beam of sunlight that now shone into the studio for a quarter of an hour at a time, every afternoon around six. Since the day before yesterday, it has also lit my upper edge on the far right. They looked out into the garden, together with me, as it were. It was a Sunday, the Sunday that the strange calendar called Palm Sunday. Lidewij had told Creator about a childhood memory of marching to the sanatorium, which was deeper in the woods surrounding Withernot. That was something they used to do on Palm Sunday when she was a girl: marching in procession from the primary school on the edge of the village, carrying decorated bamboo crosses with bread rolls shaped like roosters on them. All the grade five and six kids. Why Palm Sunday? Why did they make us do something we didn't understand? We'd carry our crosses past a row of beds with pale, drowsy kids in them, and sing a song about eggs. They'd rolled the children out onto a terrace for the occasion. The sun was still totally wintry, and we walked past singing and holding up Palm Sunday crosses. Do you understand that, Felix? What kind of celebration is that?

But Creator didn't know either. I doubt they do it these days, he said. Procter Poldermol own the sanatorium now; Fokke Ponsen wants to go live there; TB has been eradicated in the Free World; there's no call for things like that anymore.

He's picking him up next week, he said suddenly, pointing at me with his chin.

I know, Lidewij said.

And then, as if he was still talking about the same subject, Creator told her about Tijn.

He kept looking out into the garden, where the sun was sinking between the birch trunks so that, with the light coming from behind, the trunks grew blacker and blacker. Lidewij had turned on her chair to look at me — at an angle. Creator's words seemed to shed light on me, and at the same time they made me all the more aware of the absurd one-sidedness of my existence. They were talking about me and nothing but me, yet I would never know what exactly they were talking about.

How can a creature like me ever get to see itself? I was as unknowable to myself as the soul to a newborn babe: sometimes it even occurred to me that I should question whether I actually existed. Whether there was such a thing as a me. A him or a her. An it. The thing that everyone except us can see in one lightning glance. Our countenance.

When I started on Singer, Creator explained, at least fifteen years had gone by without my giving Tijn a second thought. But that very first day, I mean, after the imprimatura, when I started sketching, doing his outline to work out how to arrange him on the canvas — Singer, I mean — I realised that his penis was going to end up right in the middle. At least, twenty centimetres to the right of the middle, but optically that would become the centre of the piece. And I knew immediately that I would either paint it first before anything else or leave it until everything else was finished. I ended up leaving it till last, two days before you came back from skiing. You could say I kept putting the most difficult thing off, like always, whereas of course I still didn't have any idea why it should be difficult at all. A boy's penis isn't difficult; there's hardly a shortage of them. I could have worked from hundreds of Greek statues and even more Renaissance things and, if I'd really wanted to play it safe, I could have asked your sister for the holiday snaps of her kids — Annelise is always taking photos of the twins at the beach. And Singer's being black wasn't really the problem either; you can see that yourself.

Anyway, when all was said and done, I still hadn't come close to deciding how visible it would be, and the sheet was always there as a last resort if it proved beyond me, so ... you get the idea. I was in trouble:

I was postponing Singer's middle, because there was something I found troublesome, not technically, but ... something else. I didn't understand it, but it became more and more clear to me that the middle of the piece was just as important to me as the expression usually is, although you mustn't underestimate that either. It was immensely difficult to get Singer's eyes so that they're just the way they've turned out—so ... how can I put it ...?

So almost not looking, Lidewij said.

That, at least, was what I was hoping for, Creator said—that they would end up like that. Almost not looking. Or almost looking. But when I had more or less managed that, the day came for me to start on the middle with everything else completely finished—and then, in a flash, I knew what I should have known straightaway, from the moment I started sketching him three weeks earlier—

Creator broke off. He's no storyteller. It was obvious to me that he thought he was exaggerating it beyond redemption. He felt like shouting, Fuck psychology!

After a long silence, Lidewij asked, Does this Tijn still exist?

She had heard the name mentioned for the first time just ten minutes before and now, as she spoke it, it was as if she was touching Creator's lips.

I lost him and he lost me, Creator said. A long time ago. There's not actually anything to tell.

No? Why did you start then?

It's not what you think, Creator said. It's not something I can explain.

If you've lost someone, Lidewij said, and you still have to think about them, then it's always worth telling.

While saying this, she looked at me and smiled. Her gaze had rested momentarily on my middle, a smile had come to her lips, and then she had looked at me, at my eyes, which I now knew to be almost not looking. Or almost looking. And she winked.

Creator hadn't noticed; he was still brooding on his story and staring out at the birch wood, behind which the sun now glowed like a burning bush.

We were inseparable, Creator said, Tijn and I, for the first two years of secondary school. We found each other at lunch on the first day, immediately. We both saw immediately that we were the only ones who hadn't automatically ended up at a table with friends, and Tijn rode home with me after the last period on that very first afternoon, the way you do at that age, jumping on your bikes together and riding next to each other for a while until it's time for you to turn right for your own house, and then you keep going a bit, until there's another right, and because you're talking away and listening, you end up at the other one's house, where you decide to do your homework together, and they ask you to stay for dinner, and then you finally go home after the eight o'clock news, and then the other one rides part of the way with you, through the August evening, and every time you reach a landmark where it would make sense for him to turn around and go back home, he rides on, until the next landmark and then, somewhere exactly halfway, you reach the true point of farewell—where you have to cut the big knot, severing the strand of the newfound friendship—and you both stay standing there until you really can't stay any longer, it's getting dark, parents are worrying, they're phoning each other ... there at the halfwayest point you really are together and apart from everyone and everything else ... But, Lidewij, you have to realise that Tijn lived a full hour's bike ride from school and I lived a full hour away as well, but in the other direction, me to the west and Tijn to the east, and that we also lived a full hour away from each other—you see, our friendship was completely equilateral, and of course the next day I rode with Tijn and did my homework at his house, and I was allowed to stay for dinner, and I was happy to have Tijn ride part of the way home with me, until exactly halfway on the endless bicycle path that hugged the border between the province of Utrecht and the province of North Holland and connected my house to Tijn's.

I'm telling you this so you can understand what kind of friends we were. We wanted to be just like each other. We got the same marks, we spent the same hours in each other's company, we talked constantly—just like you and me when we're together—and we both loved drawing. There was one difference. And that was that, after almost two years, on an evening in May, in the spot halfway between our two houses, on the border of Utrecht and North Holland, Tijn suddenly asked me if I wanted to see him.

When it seemed as if the story had come to an end, Lidewij asked, Is that the way he put it? Do you want to see me?

Creator nodded. You have to realise, he said, that Tijn was by far the shyest boy in the world.

You differed in that, too, then, Lidewij said.

Not really, Creator said. But I learned to live with it, thanks to drawing. Not that I was any better at drawing than Tijn, but he never really drew from life and he definitely didn't draw people. He preferred to draw banknotes. He designed them all day long: unforgeable banknotes. And then, one evening in May, at nine o'clock in the evening, at the halfwayest point, he asked me if I wanted to see him.

Creator was silent for a moment.

If I remember correctly, we were sitting in the light of the setting sun with our backs against a tree, a bit like us now. The sun was just above the edge of the Groeneveld Castle forest—that was our spot, on the side of a field behind the castle. There were two white Fjord horses, and I think, at that moment, they were grazing next to each other's rear hooves. What I mean to say is, I was still sitting and Tijn had stood up and I was doing my very best not to look to the side, because I knew that he had lowered his pants. I kept staring ahead as much as possible, at the sun, in the direction of the tree trunks and I noticed how, with his pants around his ankles, Tijn had started jumping around to get in front of me. I think I stood up. I didn't want to look. It was as if it would scorch my eyes. Did I suspect I would see what I would see? In that instant, I heard the bell from the level crossing around the edge of the forest that the sun was setting into. I just wanted to grab my bike as fast as I could, and as I looked around for the tree we had leant our bikes against—the tree we had carved our names into two years earlier—our eyes met. I must have seen the look in his eyes as it really was, because I have always remembered it. Sometimes I think that I owe my memory for expressions to that moment … and in the end it was the look in Tijn's eyes that I thought about when I was working on Singer, do you understand … and that's the answer to your question. I was thinking of Tijn, and Tijn alone, when I tried to capture Singer.

Only now did Lidewij look away from my face. Her smile was gone, but her mouth had become as calm as a pond on a windless day. Her eyes sought my middle. She closed them and sighed. Then she took Creator's hand.

I thought about Tijn all the weeks I was working on Singer, Creator said, and I thought about how I rode home without a word. And about the next day, when it was my turn to ride home from school with him and I didn't even try to come up with an excuse. And the day after that, and the day after that, and I kept it up until there was no longer any question of our riding home with each other.

Lidewij kissed the hand she was holding.

Hey, kid, she said. Where are you now?

I knew she meant Tijn. Tijn. And me. And Felix, too, I believe. And she must have been thinking the same thing as me: the story's not over yet. There is something else to come.

Creator was fighting an inexplicable rage — at least, that was what I thought I could see.

He turned his strangely angry expression away from Lidewij and sought me out with his eyes as if I could help him. Me: a piece of linen, some paint, four stretchers, and two crossbars.

Creator had pulled his hand away from Lidewij's.

I did look at Tijn when he was standing in front of me. Very quickly. Almost without looking, I saw very well, very clearly, that — down there — he had nothing. Nothing more than ... a kind of nubble. As if half of the head of a baby's penis had been glued to the middle of his groin. And no testicles. A fingertip and nothing else — do you understand?

The sun had disappeared. The birch trunks had turned white again in the receding light.

At the word nubble, Lidewij's gaze had wandered back to my middle.

So that's why you did him like that, she said quietly.

Her hand moved imperceptibly towards me.

God, he must have loved you so much, Lidewij said, without taking her eyes off me. To want you to see him. He must have felt so safe with you.

Creator didn't answer.

Lidewij had stood up and was looking at me from straight ahead. Staring at my face. It was as if she was addressing me directly.

Fearless Fly, she said.

Specht is coming Saturday, Creator said. To pick him up.

And Lidewij said—as if it were the most logical mental leap she could make—that, as far as she was concerned, she was now perfectly certain. We're pregnant.

And she said, I never knew I could love you so terribly much, darling Felix.

As they walked out of the studio and into the house, I felt like throwing myself from the easel, tilting forwards and landing flat on the cold sunroom floor—that was how unprotected and abandoned I suddenly felt.

I wanted to shout out, What happened to Tijn?

What becomes of them? What happens to people who are no longer safe?

And I thought, Who am I? Who am I if I am Singer?

You can't let me go, Creator, not like this — not before I find out who I am. You can't dispatch me this naked. Even if he calls himself my father, the man who is coming for me on Saturday, you can't give me to him like this.

The next morning, there was a phone call from a man with a Rotterdam accent—that, at least, is what Creator told Lidewij afterwards—who had rung to pass on a message from Valery that, unfortunately, it would not be possible to pick up the painting *you have done on commission* on the agreed Saturday. Before Creator had a chance to ask why not, the voice explained that all would be clear in due course. Crystal clear.

Somehow or other, Creator had the impression he was talking to one of the shaven-headed men from the four-wheel drive.

Clear? he asked. Is something unclear?

Don't go worrying yourself, Mr Vincent. The balance will be paid in full as soon as the portrait has been picked up.

Creator hesitated. And when will that be?

Silence fell on the other end of the line. The voice seemed to be consulting with someone else, a woman, but there was mainly soughing, as if he was calling from a windy mountaintop or a yacht on the water.

We trust that you have fully kept your side of the agreement, the man said, in a tone that suggested he was answering Creator's question.

To the best of my ability, Creator replied, assuming the man was talking about the painting itself. But, he said, only Valery can know whether it's really Singer.

Singer?

A rustling silence fell in which Creator—how could it be otherwise?—was struck by a bolt of panic. He had promised not to speak to a soul about the commission ... and now he had blurted Singer's name out to a complete stranger.

Inadvertently his eyes went to the table drawer where he had stored away the Polaroid.

Suddenly the voice sounded again, and it was as if they had been carrying on a completely different conversation in the meantime.

It would be best if you prepared the painting for transportation. Packed up completely, I mean. Then we can pick it up at any time. The way things are looking now, it is extremely uncertain whether Mr Valery will be able to come in person. We will contact you the moment one of our people is in the neighbourhood.

The conversation ended without any form of goodbye, but not before the voice had said that it would be in *everyone's best interest* if Creator stuck to the agreement. To the letter.

When no one showed up on Holy Saturday, Creator wrapped me in popping paper. That's what he calls the plastic packaging material with cent-sized bubbles he uses to pack his pictures. But he couldn't bring himself to tape me up. The idea of handing Singer over not to Specht but to *one of his people* was unbearable, not just for me, but—and I was sure of this—for Creator, too.

He seemed restless and more determined than ever to adhere strictly to the terms of the agreement. I inferred this from the fact that he opened the drawer with the cheque and got out the Polaroid that he, despite the agreement, had taken of me just before Lidewij's return from skiing. He looked at it for a moment, as if it showed him something he couldn't see by looking at me, then wedged it in between my bottom stretcher and the back of my canvas. I had actually forgotten about it, the Polaroid, but now found it amusing to think that I existed a second time, wedged between canvas and stretcher, greatly reduced in size and as inaccessible to me as the far side of the moon. But still, I now existed twice, definitely.

Although I was standing with my back against a wall, the popping paper meant that all I saw for the next few months was the odd shadowy figure when someone came close in the daylight. Even listening was too much of a strain. More than anything else, my condition was one of drowsiness. In the daytime, I heard muffled sounds from the sittings, which continued uninterrupted through spring and summer. The only thing I could tell from the voices was whether the sitter was a man or a woman, and it was only towards the end of the afternoon, getting on for six, that I was able to judge from the intensity of the light whether or not the day had been sunny. Summer must have come, but the only thing I noticed was the lengthening of the days. *You have a rare skill: painting someone to life.* After the first month or two—I suspect from early June—an exceptionally long period of summery weather must have begun, because the heat became unbearable, especially after six when the sunlight started creeping slowly but surely towards me.

After the telephone conversation with the voice, Creator had applied a coat of retouching varnish and then, almost before it had dried, wrapped me up. Unsigned. I was very aware of that. It was something I had fantasised about a lot, especially the glory of it—the moment in which he would stride to my left side, from my perspective of course, to add his initials at the very bottom, in what I suspected would be a fold in the silky, pale-yellow sheet that Singer was lying on: F. V.

I had seen him do it several times on the ninety by seventies, and I admit that each time I had secretly thought, When I'm finished, he'll add more than just his initials; he'll write his name in full because, more than the others, I am the *one* thing he has dreamt of making. I am the one work in which Creator has surpassed himself—just as Specht said during that first conversation. *I realise full well that I am asking you to do something you have never done before.* These and other sentences Specht had said ran through my mind in those first weeks of my standing wrapped up to one side. *You have a rare skill: painting someone to life.* But after a while my thoughts began to die, like burnt-out embers in a fireplace. Even thoughts about the irony of my fate died—that I, who had begun as white as snow in the blackest depths of a roll and had become a dead boy, inspired by the memory of a guilty childhood memory, was again invisible, wrapped in a blind shroud, despite being bathed from wedge to wedge in the most viviparous light. Sure, I managed to prolong my consciousness for a few days by choosing colourful words like that for the few things that did run through my mind—but eventually I drowsed off on a cloud of unknowing.

To be seen is to be. I had heard Creator say that once, I think during a sitting with Cindy. I found it an arrogant thought and unphilosophical to boot—does a peacock exist more than an earthworm?—but somehow it now seemed truer to me than ever. I had existed inasmuch as Creator worked on me, and inasmuch as Lidewij was assuring herself of me. Now I started forgetting I even existed. No one had told me what an incredibly easy or smooth process that is. I tried with all my might to think about what Creator and Lidewij saw before them when they remembered me — thinking I might somehow still exist if others thought of me — but I simply couldn't imagine what they saw when they thought of me. I didn't see Tijn, I didn't see Singer, and I definitely didn't see the unborn child that had been conceived after Lidewij and Creator had stared at me with such incomprehensible delight. I didn't have the faintest notion, and my notions grew fainter and fainter.

Creator had kept to the agreement and had not shown me to a soul. My existence had been reduced to virtually nothing.

It was only last week that I woke with a start because I was being moved. For some as yet unknown reason, Creator was lifting me up on one side—I recognised his voice and Lidewij's, who was holding me on the other side. They were close enough for me to more or less understand what they were saying. Creator steered me across the studio to the cold wall, which they leant me against at a less sharp angle, so that my popping paper sagged a little and I was able to make out more of the conversation in the studio. From the words they were speaking, I gathered that Lidewij needed to be careful—easy does it, watch your back—from which I concluded not only that she was still pregnant but also, and more importantly, that there was someone else in the studio. Not another person, but another canvas. The newcomer wasn't a ninety by seventy; he had to be something bigger. I began to suspect what was going on when I heard Lidewij say that it was only now, seeing it near me, that she realised how huge it really was.

Hey, Felix, I heard Lidewij say.

She must have been on the other side of the studio, in my original location, where a huge silence now emanated from the other canvas.

Felix, when was the last time you saw Singer?

No answer came.

Don't you want to see him anymore, or is it something else?

Creator sounded testy. He was hard to understand, but I thought I heard him say that the moment had passed.

He should have been picked up, he said. That's the only way to really finish something you're making.

I heard Creator's footsteps approaching. Lidewij came closer, too.

Can I have another look at him? Just a quick one?

I felt a pang of fear, and realised that I had become a suspicious creature. What could her question mean if not that something was about to happen? My removal from the studio? My replacement by the newcomer? The arrival of two shaven-headed men with an indifferent cheque for fifty thousand euros? After so many months of indignant obscurity, I found it impossible to imagine fate smiling on me in any way at all.

Creator had pulled me towards him; my upper edge was now resting against his stomach. Carefully he peeled back the popping paper. Lidewij had come over to help unwrap me. Creator lifted me up and she jerked the paper out from under me. Then Creator used a foot to slide me closer to the wall.

There they stood, right in front of me. I blinked with what felt like Singer's eyes and, no exaggeration, felt something tingling about twenty centimetres to the left of my middle.

I don't know whether Creator looked at me. By the time I had recovered from the sudden light, he had turned his back. Demonstratively, it seemed.

Still without looking, he asked, Is it okay?

Lidewij didn't answer but nodded. She pressed her right hand against the side of her belly, which—I could see this very clearly—had grown round.

It's kicking like crazy, she said. Feel this.

Creator turned and went down on his knees before her. He pressed an ear against the spot on her belly she was pointing to.

Bloody hell, he said. It's going berserk in there.

But he didn't so much as look at me, not even later when he crossed over right in front of me to lay the popping paper in a corner of the studio.

After Creator had detached himself from her belly, Lidewij asked, Shouldn't we wrap him up again?

Leave it, Creator said. I'll do it when I get back tomorrow. Maybe I'll even leave him like that till you're back home. I won't be having any sitters for a while—not a soul will see him.

Lidewij's gaze left me. But, walking away, she turned back one last time and said, Hang in there, kid.

I remember that very well. I mean, it's not something I'm imagining because a fire is roaring outside and I'm realising that that was the last time she saw me. She said, Hang in there, kid, and it was like she was talking to herself. And she stuck up both thumbs. The gesture was new to me. Two thumbs pointing up into the air.

It will all turn out fine.

Creator had walked over to the other side of the studio and was pulling on the newcomer, as if to test its weight. Only now did I notice how strange its back was — it didn't have any crossbars, but ... What did it have? What kind of material was that? Did the newcomer have no wedges at all? I couldn't believe my eyes — it didn't even have stretchers ... How was it possible? A canvas without a frame?

It was standing; that much, I understood. Two metres tall at least; maybe two fifty. Huge.

It was painfully obvious. My successor had arrived — the new canvas on which everything would be possible, all the things Creator had not yet dared to do. And it was huger than me. It was of another order. It was ready for anything.

Oh yeah, Lidewij said, walking slowly out of the studio. I keep forgetting to tell you, someone called. I wrote her number on the back of my hand.

Who?

Minke Dupuis. She's working on a big article for

Art & Facts.

What about?

How should I know? You, maybe. She wants you to call her, otherwise she'll try again some other time.

Even before Creator and Lidewij left for the hospital, I had more or less worked out what was going on by combining the scraps of conversation that had drifted into the studio now and then. Lidewij was well into her seventh month, everything had gone smoothly, but that morning she had been in for an antenatal, at the hospital, where they had told her that, unfortunately, it would be best to play it safe. Lidewij had understood immediately which complication they were referring to; but when she tried to explain it to Creator, it remained very obscure, to me at least. What it came down to was that she would have to stay lying down until the birth, hooked up to a drip and monitored closely, and that was why they wanted to admit her to hospital. But the child was fine; that wasn't the problem.

I concluded from all of this that it must have been late October. More than half a year had passed since I had disappeared into the popping paper! And all that time, as I deduced from the conversation, there hadn't been a single sign of life from Specht or his minions. And it had been a week or two since Creator had bought the newcomer, since he'd *snapped it up*, as he put it. This was a strange expression, which he'd never used when ordering me at Van Schendel's.

FOUR

Minke on the phone: that was the first thing to happen when Creator came home from having taken Lidewij to hospital. It was getting on for five that same afternoon — it seemed an incredible coincidence.

Creator said so as well.

You calling now, that's an incredible coincidence.

She must have asked why.

Because Y is a crooked letter, Creator said.

He was wearing his dark-blue army-disposals coat. I remembered his voracious restlessness from more than six months before when, left alone in Withernot while Lidewij was off skiing, he was about to start on me.

No, I'm here by myself, he said. No, I'm not busy. Why?

Standing on the floor and leaning against the side wall of the studio, I had been able to look sideways into the garden the whole day long. The trees and shrubs were almost completely bare, which was nice for me, because it allowed me to see further into the world than usual. Between the birch trunks on the far left I could even make out a glimmer from the lake, there where the sunset would be just visible to the right of the wall opposite. While the sun was going down, long oblique shadows teemed across the yellowing lawn. The reeds at the end of the garden had turned rusty and were topped with plumes that, in this light, looked almost lilac. I felt like I was looking with Creator's eyes — by which I mean, slurping it all up as if my eyes were digesting everything they could see, as if I had become some kind of visual maw.

Last year, Lord Peacock had appeared here, the day that I came within a hair's breadth of becoming Cindy. I realised suddenly that it had been months since I had heard his cry or his scratching in the bowl of chicken feed.

I say I, but of course I mean we: Singer and I. But it was as if Singer had never existed. I remembered things he had never seen — things like Lord Peacock, from before his existence. I remembered the things he couldn't possibly know. It was strange to be there in deathly quiet Withernot like that, and forgetting that I was painted. Yes, in that hour, I felt like I was blank, a novice on whom anything could happen.

It was because of the other canvas; I realised that clearly.

So this is what people mean when they say they are shy.

There was nothing I wanted more than to have the other look at me, and at the same time I feared his gaze.

I did my very best not to look at him, not even the back of him, for all that he was standing there directly opposite me, strange and stretcherless.

It was so quiet that I heard Creator's car coming from a long way away — the approaching drone of the engine on the narrow, twisting cart track through the woods between Huizen and Old Valkeveen. He must have felt strange. I tried to imagine it: suddenly wifeless, anxiously awaiting the birth of his child, facing an unexpected period of several weeks' solitude, with a new huge canvas, and no appointments with sitters or clients ... How could he be in anything other than his now-or-never mood? It was the same as when he made me, Lidewij had been away then, too.

He came into the studio with a black plastic bag. I recognised the bag because it didn't have anything printed on it. All the bags of the Free World have a coloured logo. Only bags like this — the kind he had come back with seven months ago as well, after taking Lidewij to Schiphol — are unprinted and black. I knew what would emerge from it: carefully packaged videotapes. Creator would remove the videotapes and throw away the covers — quickly, as if he found them unpleasant. Last time, I was able to look at one of the covers for most of a minute out of the corner of one of my eyes, curious as I am about supports, whether they are made of linen, like me, or plastic. The video cover was called *Fiona on Fire* and showed a frontal view of a naked blonde woman straddling a naked man. Her mouth was half open so that somehow you looked deep into it, and she was weighing me up. I think that's how you put it. There was a weighing-up look in her eyes. I wondered whether Creator thought she looked like Lidewij. I didn't — she was more like Cindy. Still, there was something forthright about her expression that could make you think of Lidewij.

That might have been why Creator didn't throw her away immediately, because of that expression. For the rest he hid the videos, now coverless, at the bottom of the wicker basket where he dumped his old paint rags. Now and then he would get them out at night to play them in the adjoining room. I was never really a party to it. Looking through the doorway, I knew that Creator was sitting there to the left of one jamb, while, to the right of the other, a television screen must have been showing more or less what was promised by the cover. That, at least, was what I assumed. In time I was able to predict from certain noises, basically groaning and straining, when Creator's viewing would end. I always noticed that he never deigned to look at me when, still hoisting up his jeans, he came to hide the videos at the bottom of the wicker basket afterwards.

It could be my imagination, but I'm pretty sure he was even trying to avoid my gaze.

Minke had called while the black plastic bag was still dangling from his wrist. When it became clear that she would be coming that same evening, Creator buried the bag under the rags in the basket without inspecting its contents. It had grown dark: an enormous, night-black cloud had slid down from the direct north to cover the sky. For the first time in my existence, Creator lowered the venetians in front of the sliding doors. A few of the slats were bent; he clicked them straight. Then he collected a few lamps from other rooms and very carefully placed them in strategic positions around the studio. I noticed that he was keeping me in the shadows. He disappeared again, upstairs this time—I heard him bumping around in one of the rooms I would never see as long as I lived—and came back with a mattress, which he put down close to the newcomer and covered with a plaid blanket. Now and then he looked at me, while bustling around, and it was almost as if he was winking. Laidback, huh? We're making it tremendously atmospheric.

Creator covered the lamps with scarfs and cloths so that the room was awash with a dim glow, then went to fetch an apple-green silk shawl from the hall of Withernot, where they hung up the coats. He opened it out completely, turning it into a wide, flimsy veil, and draped it over me, hiding the darkened sunroom from my view. I had a strong impression that, in this light, I too was completely hidden. All I could see of Creator at this stage was a greenish shadow.

Creator is, as he puts it, not so much someone who looks as someone who arranges. Before I can see what I want to paint, he sometimes tells his sitters, I have to arrange the world I see before me like a film director. I have seen him arranging people like that many times, putting them in the pose he wants to capture on canvas — and I know how much his desire to create something is spurred by his directing. Watching the video of Singer, he had paused him in just the same way. And I have often wondered what exactly happens in the neighbouring room when he watches his videos. I have heard him pausing the picture with the magical device he calls the remote control and often loses, the same device he also uses to fast-forward or switch to slow motion. What kind of power does he have in moments like this? Which orders does he give? Does Creator only really feel that he is a creator when he is freezing naked people with his remote control? What does this desire want from him?

I'll pick you up at the station, Creator had told Minke. After dark, Withernot is completely impossible to find.

If they made small talk, they did it in the car, because when they came into the studio they were talking about *Palazzo*.

If I'd known you were going to find it so horribly embarrassing, that bit about the Pietà, I would have dropped it, I heard the low husky voice say, suddenly remembering it perfectly.

I thought it actually says something, about you, about how you see your work, and —

She interrupted herself.

Wow, she said.

Evidently she was now in the studio, in a darker spot, because through my veil I couldn't make her out at all.

I always turn everything around to face the wall, Creator said.

Except that, she said.

She meant me. I heard her walking towards me.

Is this the same canvas as —

Why didn't Creator say anything?

So you didn't turn it into a Pietà after all, she said teasingly. She laughed. Then it would have been upright, wouldn't it?

Presumably, Creator nodded.

Hmmm, she said. Do I get to see it? It's been quite a while since I saw a Vincent.

I had the impression she didn't believe Creator when he mumbled that I wasn't finished yet.

It's a bit black over Bill's mother's, Creator said.

What?

It's an expression—it means it's going to pour.

He was trying to distract her. I knew that technique of his well; he talked like that sometimes when he had sitters, too.

A silence fell.

Your wife, isn't she here?

She's gone away for the week.

Creator was thinking, as if he'd been asked something else as well.

She's gone to her aunt's. Aunt Drea, her mother's sister.

Why did he turn his evasion into an outright lie?

Now it was apparently Minke's turn to change the subject.

And that, what's that going to be?

She had turned her back on me and meant the newcomer.

That's not a canvas, Creator said.

I can see that, she said.

I snapped it up at an auction.

I could tell from the way he was standing that he had pulled the newcomer back from the wall.

Wow, Minke said. Why don't you turn it around?

If you help, Creator said.

They were now standing on either side of the newcomer. He must have been unusually heavy, because they had to strain to lift him up. First they put him on his side, so that he was horizontal, then they turned him around.

It cost next to nothing, Creator said, panting. Because of the — what do you call it? — flaking.

He gestured.

Through the veil I couldn't see what the newcomer represented. He was horizontal, after all! And there could be someone painted on him. A reclining figure — but I could only see my own, flimsy apple-green.

I had been prepared for many things, but not Creator allowing a thing by somebody else into his studio.

But that's not what you're here for, Creator said. What would you like me to tell you?

He was standing at the oak table, which, thanks to one of the lamps, was relatively brightly lit, and gestured for Minke to sit down.

Glass of wine?

D'you have white?

Creator walked out of the sunroom. Minke jumped up and strode over to me. She lifted the veil on my right—at my feet, in other words—and kept lifting it until she saw the spot twenty centimetres to the right of my middle. I tried to make out her expression through the veil, but her face was hidden behind a fold. The only detail I caught a glimpse of was her platinum-blonde hair—although I remembered it as copper red. In that same instant she let go of me and hurried back to the table. Creator came in with a bottle of wine and two glasses.

She doesn't know that, right this moment, Lidewij is in hospital, I thought; she doesn't even know that Lidewij is expecting a baby. God knows what else Creator is keeping her in the dark about as well.

I think there might be some nuts somewhere, he said.

He sounded nervous.

No, thanks, she said. And to hide her agitation she decided to go straight to the point.

Do you mind if I smoke?

I was the only one who heard that she was out of breath.

Creator got up and took a small box from under the easel.

Use this for the ash.

She had seen my feet. My legs, my knees, my

thighs, my waist. She had been unable to restrain a short, sharp sigh, like a gasp. And she had dropped the veil, as if it had burnt her fingers. She lit a cigarette.

It's about Valery, she said. I'm working on a major portrait of him. For the newspaper. Quite revealing. Sensational facts. There are a few things I'm trying to find out. I already know most of it. And it suddenly occurred to me: as far as I know, you're the last person he saw.

Specht, Creator said hesitantly. I noticed he was being cautious. From the direction of his voice, I could tell that he had looked at me for a moment.

You know some other Valery? Minke laughed.

I thought, She laughs like a man, with that husky voice of hers.

The paper's going to publish it, my article, the moment he's dead. That's why I'm under so much pressure now.

Dead?

Creator gasped, seemingly for the same breath as me.

Didn't you know?

And she told the astonished Creator what she knew. Incurable disease, a cancer that had been proliferating for years — that was why he went through phases of being completely bald. And now, after more than a year of intensive treatment, he had, according to her best sources, lost consciousness and was dying, if he wasn't already dead. That was why he'd come to Rotterdam from Antibes; he was at the Erasmus Medical Centre. It really was a question of hours; she knew that for a fact.

After an extended silence, Creator asked, When was the last time *you* saw him then?

I think it was a couple of weeks after he came here.

Specht, here?

I could feel Creator's brain racing. Since the telephone call from the Bald Man, as he called him, so long ago now, he had realised that *the agreement* was not a game.

What are you playing dumb for? Valery was here — he told me that himself.

Himself?

I was sure Creator was thinking the same thing as me: Minke is trying to test me.

She scowled. What difference does it make? He'll be dead either today or tomorrow. And then you'll get an avalanche of obituaries and articles. And facts. And you, according to my best sources, are the last person he met with.

No. That would be you then, Creator said.

Okay, me then.

A silence fell.

Brilliant wine, she said.

I heard the glasses being refilled — this time by

Minke, I think.

I don't know what you're being so ridiculously secretive about, Minke said. There's no law against seeing Specht.

Creator cleared his throat. Only now did I notice that he, too, had taken the news very badly. He could hardly speak.

Did he know he was dying?

For more than a year now, Minke said.

So that was it, I thought; that was what we saw. The beads of sweat, the failing voice, the distraught emptiness appearing in his eyes every now and then ... when Specht was here commissioning Creator, he knew that he was carrying out his last acts ... mercy, spare me ... and those three sessions, when he tried to conjure Singer up before Creator's eyes ... perhaps they were his last great effort ...

I didn't know, Creator said. I had no idea. *Pas du tout.*

And he said, God, how could I be so blind?

He kept finding it hard to grasp what he had just heard from Minke.

You'll be saving a life.

What?

Nothing, Creator said, nothing.

He was bewildered. Never before had I felt so strongly that I was going through the same thing as him. I, too, was bewildered.

Minke stubbed out her cigarette. What's that noise?

It's started raining, Creator said. As promised.

A broad rustling had started up in the garden.

The commission, I thought. The commission. It was Specht who commissioned me! He was going to pick me up and see me! Then and only then would I know who I am now that I'm Singer. *Who* will I belong to if I can't belong to the man who commissioned me?

What did he come here for?

Valery?

I don't know why you're being so ridiculously cautious, Minke said. What difference does it make now? Any moment now, we're liable to hear he's dead, and you're one of the last people who saw him. Why be so difficult?

Minke had stood up. I heard her walking towards me. Creator had stood up as well, abruptly. A glass of wine fell to the floor, shattering. I smelt the sour smell.

Don't, Creator said.

I think he stopped her hand just as it was about to lift my veil.

There was more between them than just the tension between someone who wanted to see something and someone who wanted to stop them.

You can see him, Creator said. One condition: not a soul finds out.

Why not? Minke had giggled for a moment, because of the word *soul*.

Not a soul, Creator repeated. I promised.

He was the one who pulled back the veil.

Do you promise, you haven't seen this?

Did he see her nod?

For a moment, we exchanged glances, Creator and I. His was imploring; the blood had drained from his face. Then he turned and started clearing away the glass.

Minke was standing to my left, near my head. In this light, her eyes looked brown, but I knew they were green.

The thing I had grown more or less accustomed to happened: her gaze lingered on my face for just a moment before it was drawn to my middle. Where it became a stare.

But this wasn't what struck me, even if I had seen at a glance that her long hair really had turned blonde and her arms were bare, in a tight, tomato-red, shoulderless top, with a shoelace-like band around her long neck.

It wasn't the sight of Minke that struck me like a bolt of lightning. It was the newcomer, directly opposite me. Now that the green veil had been pulled aside I could finally, finally see him. And he was enormous — a life-sized reclining nude, stretched out from head to toe on a background of satin-green folds. There was hardly any light on him, but I still noticed that my gaze was drawn not to his face but to his middle. There had to be something to see there, but there was some trick of the light ... there was *no light*, or so it seemed, in that spot, because of the lamps, which Creator had set up wrongly. No matter how hard I looked, it was like gazing into a hole.

Wow, Minke said.

She had moved right over in front of me. She took two solemn steps towards me. Now she was blocking the newcomer; I tried to look around her, but could only see his feet.

A single thought filled my mind: He's seen me.

The other has seen me.

It was as if Singer was getting warm from his feet to the top of his head, a glow spreading over his entire body.

This could be blushing.

The rustling in the garden had grown deeper, heavier, a curtain of sound closing us off from the outside world.

I believe that if I had been a person I would have now felt like vomiting. From excitement. Let me look, was all I thought; let me see what I just missed out on seeing. I didn't get a proper look; give me another chance, then I'll see what I forgot to see — how he looks at me, the expression in the other's eyes when I am looking.

And there was something else I thought.

How alone he is, I thought. How can someone be so terribly alone?

Somehow I knew that, in thinking this, I was thinking something that only people can think.

But Minke was standing between us, and Creator, whose hands smelt of wine, had come over to stand next to her, and outside the rain rustled.

Creator had lit a cigarette, which he now inserted between Minke's lips.

How did you manage that?

She stretched out a hand, with the cigarette, and pointed at my middle.

Creator smiled.

She hesitated, If you hadn't said it was a boy …

Did I say that?

You said *he*. That's what you said. *He*.

Minke licked her lips without thinking and brushed her hair back with a few long swipes of her free hand. Creator had laid his left hand on the back of her neck, under her hair. She took him by the wrist with her free hand, brushing me with her elbow, just above my face.

You're still a lefty, she said.

Yep, he said.

They looked.

Who is he?

Does it matter?

Say who I am, I thought. Tell Minke that I am your commission, that you accepted me.

You will be saving a life.

Those six words had always baffled me and now, as Creator drew his gaze away from me and moved his mouth towards Minke's hair, to her ear, I could only think one thing. I thought, Don't let go of me now.

Promise, Creator whispered, with his mouth against her hair. Promise you won't tell anyone about it.

She, too, looked away from me now, although keeping her grip on his wrist, and turned her face to his. She was taller than him, I saw that now: she bent her legs a little.

Whether it was her mouth seeking his or his seeking hers, I don't know.

Hi, Creator said, hardly pulling back from her at all.

So you still taste of that, he said. Of Gauloises.

She laughed briefly and asked, Where were we?

She threw the cigarette on the floor. Creator stubbed it out with the toe of his shoe.

I hadn't seen it this close up before, the incomprehensible thing called touch, two mouths together. I was pretty sure that what was happening between them now was different from what had happened between Lidewij and Creator more than six months ago; this was more breathless, more panicky too, as if they were suddenly pursued by God knows who or what, as if any interruption of the touching and gestures that followed one after the other in a kind of hectic flood could cause a lull that would be as fatal to them as a thorn to a bubble. For a moment, Creator pulled back from Minke's mouth — I saw that his was redder than before — and said, He's dead.

With her mouth still seeking his, Minke asked, Who?

Him, Creator said, gesturing at me with his chin. When I painted him he was dead.

He spoke slowly. He sounded somehow triumphant. As if saying *dead* would make Minke move even closer to him.

What's he called? she asked, as his mouth covered hers again.

To my left, not far from the sliding door, a drop fell. I had heard it a few times earlier; there's a leak there.

Creator hadn't answered.

For a moment, it seemed as if Minke was about to disentangle herself, but she stopped the pushing movement — that was a decision, I saw that very clearly — and Creator grabbed the bottom hem of her top and peeled it up over her belly, her stomach, her breasts, her throat, her face, her long arms — a lightning movement she made possible by going down on her knees with arms raised. While Creator strode away from her to the mattress, which he dragged over to the middle of the room, exactly between me and the newcomer, she unhooked her bra, pushed down her skirt, and stepped out of her knickers. Red pumps, black nylon stockings, a shoelace around her neck: it was as if she'd been studying the cover of one of Creator's videos. It was also as if she knew what the two of them had to do. How can I put it, I had the impression I was seeing something that had already taken place, something they were staging. Creator had lain down on his back on the mattress, with his head to the newcomer and his feet, still in his shoes, to me. He had slid his jeans and underpants down to his knees and held his head up to look at her while she, with her back to me, walked towards him.

To my left, the drops fell every other second, but Creator didn't do what he did otherwise; he didn't slide a bucket under the leak.

Where were we?

Here, Minke said. In front of the mirror.

She was now standing at Creator's feet.

I'm not free, remember. You always ask how much it costs.

How much does it cost?

They sounded like a couple of kids working out the rules of a game.

That depends.

On what?

On what you want, you know that.

125

And what do I want?

You know very well what you want.

And how much is that going to cost me?

Minke took a breath and gestured backwards, meaning me.

What do you say to ... something like what you got for him.

She laughed, kicked off her pumps, and knelt down beside him.

Is that all? I could see that Creator was doing his best not to touch her.

You haven't changed a bit, she said. For God's sake, what have we been doing in the meantime?

If I had kept paying attention I would have undoubtedly understood exactly what they meant, where they had been, exactly what the game they were playing meant—once, and when, and now, at this actual moment—but it was as if a black haze had descended before my eyes. Absurd imagery for an Extra Fine Quadruple Universal Primed but, for quite a while, it really was as if I had been struck blind.

Here. In front of the mirror.

Those were Minke's words.

Mirror.

In. Front. Of. The. Mirror.

That was the newcomer.

He was me.

That, him, there, on the other side of the room, directly opposite me — he wasn't looking at me. He was me. He was exactly who I was. This was it, that looking *in*.

Between him and me, Minke straddled Creator's thighs, blocking my view of my middle. I understood perfectly well what *that* meant: she was sitting opposite herself, she too was now looking *in* — and I imagined her expression as more or less the same as Fiona's weighing-up look, On Fire — while making careful little movements with her hands down under her belly, as if stroking a small animal. I also realised that Creator was looking at her, just as she was looking at herself in the mirror. At least, my gaze grazed the side of Minke's waist and caught a glimpse of Creator's face, which was lost in looking at hers. I knew this expression: it was his discriminating look, the one that kept people at a distance. He was trying with all his might to keep watching and not disappear into bliss, and Minke was trying to do that, too, while watching her reflection from a distance, even while lowering her torso very firmly onto the part of Creator I had only seen once before — the time he'd left his mobile phone on the easel and got an unexpected call while watching the videos from the black bag.

I hardly saw any of this because I was trying to see myself, my face that was staring at me to the right of Minke's ribs, out of the semi-darkness of the mirror, which, as I now realised, really was swathed in mist — it was sown with golden-brown flakes — and, no matter how I try, I will not be able to describe my expression. Every time I felt I had composed myself enough to finally see it, restlessness overwhelmed me again. Close your eyes, I thought. Don't see this. Listen to the drops instead, to the dark rain rustling outside. This isn't meant for human eyes — we aren't made to see what we are. Somehow or other I knew that this, finally, was my own expression — that Creator had wanted to capture me like this, *so not yet knowing what I was seeing.* He had laid me down on a womb of the greenest satin and outside, on Crete's warmest pebble beach, he had imagined children's voices, he had filled me with Tijn, with the memory of looking away and not wanting to see, of realising yet being unaware. Creator had wanted to capture me in that last solitary moment in which we look up from our innocence because we want to know who we are in the eyes of the world.

Minke's movements had grown more intense; she had planted her hands on Creator's shoulders. They didn't make a single noise, at least not with their voices — all I heard was the flapping splash of their bodies and the drops and the rain.

Look, Creator said. Look as long as you can.

Had Minke stopped looking?

She interrupted her movement, swung her hair back, and turned around without raising her haunches off Creator.

Now she was sitting opposite me.

Who is he, Felix?

She was looking at me from straight ahead, and her eyes glided over my entire surface, from toes to thighs to stomach to face.

Singer, Creator groaned. Valery's son.

She froze.

I am sure that, for an instant, I saw her smile. As if her face—grown glassy and hard from all that looking, with lips squeezed tight—had melted for a moment. It was perhaps the smallest imaginable change in her face, and yet it immediately made her indescribably sad.

Don't stop, for God's sake, Creator said.

He tried to keep the rhythm going with thrusting movements, but Minke grew more and more immobile.

Creator thrust on, as if trying to keep time to the drops.

What did you say he was called?

What difference does it make?

Singer, she said. You called him Singer.

And to herself she said, voicelessly—I read her lips—*Slave*.

She had pulled away from Creator. He took his penis in his left hand and kept moving in the same rhythm.

Valery's son, she said. That's what you said. Valery's son.

And she whispered, Oh God, the deceit, the deceit. He buys a slave and calls him his son.

Her voice had turned shrill.

How much did you get for him?

Only now did I see that Creator, while accelerating his movements, was looking at me and contracting strangely from neck to knees, as if trying to bunch his body into a fist. He groaned. I think at the word *slave*. His groan was the first cry of pleasure to come from his throat since it started, there on the mattress, and something sprayed out of his penis, which, it seemed to me, had turned an unnatural purple. Something milky and fluffy oozed up — a substance that was, more than anything, helplessly impotent.

Creator fell backwards, both hands covering his penis.

You don't talk about that, do you? No, you never talk about money.

She still hadn't looked back.

How did he die?

Creator tried to pull her towards him by her ankle, but she stepped free of his grip. She was now avoiding my eyes; that was plain to see.

I don't know, Creator said. It was as if he had hardly heard a word of what she had just said. He was panting.

What do you mean, you don't know?

Minke's voice had got louder, shriller.

You said he was dead—you said that yourself. You must know how he died.

No, Creator said. Come on, please.

He had stood up.

God knows where he got him from. Now she was shouting, still looking at me. As if she didn't want to know what had happened behind her.

She shouted and sounded derisive.

I thought he only got them from Morocco.

I don't know what you mean, Creator said. He was his son.

Minke laughed out loud. Jeering, she sounded even hoarser and shriller.

You're not going to tell me you believed him—you're not that naïve.

Creator didn't answer. He had released his penis and closed his knees.

Whose son? For years, Valery has lived as lonely as a ...

She searched for a comparison.

As a wolf, she said.

She gestured at me.

How many paintings like this do you think he's had made over the years? ... Always the latest boy. Always an artist he *actually* considered beneath him. Always the boy who was suddenly that little bit too old to get him going. But hell, this really was the last one, I presume.

Her voice had grown tight with contempt.

Defend me, I thought. Creator, why don't you defend me? Why don't you scream at her that I'm the only one, the son, the child who found and received Specht's protection in the compound next to the swimming pool in Sierra Leone? Tell her about Tijn, about Lidewij, about the baby that's on its way, about all the hours when you only wanted one thing — painting someone to life, making a person, making Singer, becoming a creator.

But Creator held his tongue, like someone who knows he stinks.

She gestured at her throat.

It's a question of hours, over there at the Erasmus Medical Centre.

She strode through the room to gather up her clothes, and started dressing.

Perverts, she said — not to Creator in particular, by the sound of it.

I was the only one who had noticed that it had stopped raining and that only dripping was audible.

What got into me? I've made a horrible mistake.

She gave a grim smile.

You going to stick to it — him being dead? You going to keep wallowing in those crocodile tears?

Creator looked confused. A truth seemed to be

dawning on him. Once again, I seemed to catch on faster than he did.

I'm not dead, I thought. Surely not, surely not.

I, Singer, lying here opposite my reflection, draped over a satin sheet, I am still alive.

Nobody's going to believe you, Minke said. That he was dead when you painted him. That's not even possible—you only work from life, real Cindys, that's what you work from … you yourself put it so beautifully: It's only possible from life.

She stepped into her pumps. She sounded scornful.

Does Lidewij find it beautiful as well? So moving, so innocent? Her voice had turned to steel.

It's stupid that I always say sorry. Sorry. I'm even worse than—

With one gesture, she took in all of Withernot.

But I don't accept every job that's offered to me. Specht couldn't have asked me anything he liked, the way he apparently could with you.

She sounded triumphant.

That was all last night.

A half-hour ago, Creator built a pyre at the bottom of the garden, down by the reeds. It was still twilight. The sliding doors are open; I can hear the fire crackling. The wind is still blowing from the north. Sparks shoot up out of the smoke, drift towards the studio, and float in as flakes of ash. Creator grabbed the video of Singer and the snaps he got from Specht, and took them out to the fire. He came back without the video or snaps. Then he walked over to the basket with paint rags and pulled out the other videos. I don't really know what they've got to do with it, but he went and threw them on the fire, too. I can now smell the acrid, toxic smell of melting plastic. After that, I was sure he was going to walk up to me, with his bewildered expression and unruly hair.

I'm coming to a tragic end — that was, more or less literally, what I thought. And it was as if the world flashed before me: from the roll at Van Schendel's, past the day they carried me into the studio, Cindy and Specht and Tijn and Lidewij, up to and including Minke. I was aware of it all — not as a story, I don't think, more as a tightly bunched knot of time that suddenly, with an incredible tug, had come undone.

I don't know how long it kept dripping. Creator got dressed and they walked out of the studio, one after the other, with hardly another word.

Once she was out in the hall, I heard Minke say, You're sticking to your story, aren't you—that you haven't been paid for that boy?

Creator will have answered evasively; I know him inside out.

He's used to paying, Minke said. It's all he knows—he pays for everything. God knows what he pays for his slaves in that horrible fucking country.

Outside I heard the car start and drive off with the sound of splashing. There are potholes out there in the track they call the drive. Every time it rains, Creator resolves to really do something about them. The wind had come up. There was no doubt of that; I heard the gusts blow drops against the sliding doors.

Somehow or other, Creator had been sensible enough to slide a bucket under the leak. They wanted to cover themselves like Adam and Eve; they wanted to be invisible. And they didn't want to be a couple—anything but that.

It was an iron bucket, as old as Withernot itself. The handle rattled and the drops fell with shrill echoes until a layer of water had built up. After a while, the drops fell at intervals as long as a drawn-out thought. Plip. Plop.

On his way out, Creator had turned off the lamps. The presence of mind of people—it mystifies me. He looked at me for a moment, with Minke already out in the hall.

He cursed. I had the impression he was cursing me. He cursed again.

Specht dying—maybe already dead—the man who had wanted me to exist, who had commissioned Creator to make me. It was because of Specht that Creator had dredged Tijn up out of his memory. Because of Specht that I had my expression, and a nose that wasn't too flat, and a skin of burnt umber, caput mortuum, and cadmium yellow, a middle that tingled, and a hand without a thumb. Because of Specht that Lidewij, this very afternoon, had stared at my middle and unconsciously rubbed her big, round belly. It was because of Specht that that belly had grown big and round. Because of no one but Specht. It was for Specht that I existed.

Where was he? Where is a human who is dying?

Specht was the only one who could see the life in me, the life I was meant to have. I suddenly realised that. There was only one person who could locate me, by seeing me and saying, Ah, Singer, there you are, and now you're no longer as dead as always, you are what you are—and that was Specht.

I know that I should have felt abandoned. It would have made me seem human; people would have been able to identify with me, through my saying, Now I am all alone; Specht is dead and I am a canvas alone with Singer.

But there was something.

There was a presence.

Some part of me was being reflected. It had to be, I knew it had to be, somewhere across from me, in the now fully invisible mirror. I know that this thought calmed me. At least, I imagined that the world was full of completely invisible mirrors that retained a memory of what they had reflected.

I even thought, I am one of those mirrors.

I preserve someone's likeness.

I, the support.

It didn't really help. I'm no philosopher—my thoughts only ever calm me for a moment, and I simply don't have the strength to be my own creator. The questions, fears, and tremblings came rushing in from all sides.

I tried to tell myself that I was still alive.

Even if Specht is dying in the faraway EMC, there is still one person who will see me, sometime, and that one person knows who I am. I clung to Minke's words despite knowing better, because what could she know of Singer? Still, she had snapped at Creator, You going to stick to it—him being dead? You going to stick to those crocodile tears?

Nobody is going to believe him; I now understood that much. Soon, when Specht is dead, they will get to see me—people, strangers, individuals as derisive as Minke—and they will say, That's one of Specht's slaves. He paid big money for him in a ruined, war-ravaged country and brought him to Creator's studio and got him to paint him for him, here; he only ever works from life; he could never make something he couldn't see before him …

It's possible, I thought forcefully, as if my entire existence depended on that one thought. What Minke said could be true. Whatever else has happened to Singer—it could be true that he's not dead. God knows what kind of game Specht wanted to play with Creator … What does it matter, if *he* is still alive?

Creator came back three-quarters of an hour later. The dripping had stopped; a rising wind had swept the skies clean. Creator didn't show himself in the studio again, except to give in to an illogical craving for order by raising the venetians in the dark. The moon was out—you could tell from the pale, seething shadows in the garden.

I was able to look at myself again in the half-light of morning: I was a dark, unfathomable patch on a colourless background of folds. On the floor between me and my likeness was the mattress, close to the bucket, which was standing in a puddle of water. By now, the wind had become a real gale, blasting straight onto the sliding doors, but I could see that the sky was cloudless.

Everything around Withernot rustled and shrieked. I think that was why I didn't hear the sound of the car until it drove in through the garden gate. A car door shut, light hasty footsteps came down the drive, a woman's footsteps sounded and, during a brief lull in the wind's howling, a thud was audible in the hall. I knew that sound—I heard it every morning before

Creator walked into the studio with the newspaper. But this wasn't the newspaper. I heard the car door again. Almost immediately, the ignition sounded and the car raced off, to be drowned out by the storm a few seconds later. In the same instant, Creator stumbled around upstairs, he drummed down the staircase, and opened the front door.

Minke! he shouted. Minke, come back!

A strong draught had come up in the studio — the popping paper in the corner rustled and slid — like a cold breath blowing across my whole surface. The front door banged shut. The studio calmed instantly.

Immediately afterwards, Creator came in holding an envelope.

He had already torn it open and was reading the first lines of a letter out loud, as if on the stage: Felix, this is the article that will appear in *Art & Facts* as soon as Specht is dead. Everything has been checked and double-checked. I had it with me last night to show it to you, but nothing went the way I expected. I wanted to give it to you. I don't understand what happened, either. Forgive me — suddenly you were so completely the Felix from the old days; no one looks at me the way you look at me. But when you said who it was in the painting — read it, please, and don't be shocked, and forgive me. The article is the truth and nothing but.

Creator was wearing the same clothes as a few

hours earlier; he even still had his spattered shoes on. He must have flopped onto his bed without getting undressed. Standing between me and my reflection, he unfolded several sheets of typed paper. I could see clearly that there had been a few prints in the envelope — colour prints. One of them floated down to the floor. Creator was absorbed by what he was reading. More than ever, I realised that I was completely at the mercy of coincidence; there was no other way I could begin to understand the gist of Minke's article. Creator ignored the print that had floated away.

During one of the sittings with the charismatic hypnotherapist's children, I had heard Creator discussing the Internet with the oldest of the three boys. You could be *on* it and you could download whatever you liked. This was one of those things — a print from the Internet, a photo, lying, from my perspective, upside down. I could see just enough to make out a human figure. But that was enough to send a mad chill to my heart. It was someone dark-skinned, there on the paper.

When he had finished the letter, he spent a long time staring straight ahead, more or less at the popping paper, without seeing anything, without moving, seemingly without even breathing.

So it's true, he said. He groaned.

I got the impression he wanted to vomit. His

Adam's apple seemed to have developed a life of its own—he swallowed frantically for a while, then disappeared into the living room.

The wind he made turned the print on the floor around, giving me a better view.

It was a boy, black—as I had thought—naked, and lying on a bed. His eyes were closed.

Is he me? I thought.

And I knew it. This was Singer. This was me.

Now I heard the television; Creator had turned it on. Out of my sight, he walked from the living room to the toilet. I think he was trying to vomit, but that didn't happen, and when he came back into the room the first news item had started.

What was he expecting to hear? The Erasmus Medical Centre has just announced the death, after a long illness, of the Rotterdam dredging baron Valery Specht, reputedly the Netherlands' richest man, a renowned art collector and connoisseur of underage boys, who leaves behind a global real-estate empire?

It was only about a war that would be waged as soon as the rest of the world grasped how dangerous the dictator was.

Creator switched off the TV.

It came as no surprise to me that the first thing he thought of now was the cheque. He pulled it out of the drawer in the big table, from between the pencil stubs and the paperclips. I don't know what he was staring at now—the signature perhaps, the only direct proof, here in the studio, of Specht's existence? He laid the cheque on the table and picked the print up off the floor. I could see his face now: it was as if his hair was standing on end, as if he'd walked through the storm outside. His lips were pressed together, as if he was forcing himself to keep a cool head.

He laid the envelope, the letter, and the prints—about five of them, by the look of it—on the table next to the cheque. Then he walked to the mirror opposite me, and turned it upright and around, so that its light-grey, crazed back was facing me again. Creator's actions had become determined: he strode over to the video projector, which was on its stand just next to the popping paper, moved it over next to me, and turned it on. Then he pulled out a video. I recognised it immediately—it was Specht's video of Singer. He put it into the VCR and aimed the lens at the greyish-white back of the mirror.

It wasn't my idea, becoming human. But one day I was taken away from Van Schendel's, as from a distant continent, by a man who wanted to make me human. He paid money for me—I cost substantially more than double weave, and my stretchers are glued, all of three point six. I don't know where it came from, the longing I started to feel here in Withernot. I don't know, but it arose within me, not like a thought, but like a wind that starts to blow unnoticed. I had no choice but to want what Creator wanted; I had never longed for anything as intensely as I longed to be Singer, to live, and to feel the gaze of anyone at all who, seeing me, would say, He looks real—look, a person, Singer.

None of this was my idea, and yet I must now feel what people feel. I am even fated to feel the last thing they feel—I must feel the out-of-control terror they feel, how irrationally desperate fear makes them.

Creator was completely overcome by fear. I'm dead, he thought. If the world sees what I now see, everyone will think I'm the biggest sleazebag imaginable … The outrage, the outrage … No one will ever sit for me again … Withernot, Withernot will never be ours …

Lidewij, I heard him whispering — if Lidewij sees this … But still he projected the video of Singer on the back of the mirror. He already knew everything, but he still wanted to see it.

That was how I came to see him in full before me for the first time, the video of Singer, with the children playing just outside the sunny window, with the boat from Chora Sfakion blowing its horn, with the motionless dark body that started it all. Creator froze the picture, and the sound of summer died. Creator clicked ahead a couple of times until the stripes disappeared from the picture, and then he looked at the prints. One after the other, he compared the prints to what he saw in front of him in the studio, and his gaze lingered the longest on one of the prints — the one that had floated down to the floor.

Fuck, he said.

He dumped the papers on the table and ran out of the studio.

By the sound of it, the vomiting was successful this time; I heard an infernal hawking sound and the flush of the toilet.

All that time I stared at Singer — frozen, crackled Singer, lying on the bed of a bygone summer.

After returning, Creator adjusted the projector to bring Singer's face closer and closer. I don't know if Creator could already see what he wanted to see.

Singer's enlargement took on monstrous proportions, and then Creator let the picture go. That's the word—he pressed a button that somehow interrupted the freezing of the magnified face. The picture moved, but it wasn't Singer who was moving; it was the person who was watching, the camera itself. Singer didn't even seem to be breathing.

Oh, God, Creator said.

Dead.

Did he say it out loud?

Generally, I was the first to understand what Creator needed to understand, but this time he was very obviously ahead of me. He was capable of considering a possibility that was somehow beyond my comprehension.

He was capable of thinking Singer dead.

That was it.

He saw Singer dead.

He had already understood, and now he saw. With his own two eyes.

All those weeks he'd spent looking at the video footage while preparing for the painting, he hadn't been able to. He hadn't needed to, either. He hadn't wanted to.

But now he could clearly think it.

This, this video recording, is Singer dead.

I've worked from death.

He couldn't think anything else; I realised that.

Everything he had read in Minke's article seemed to bring him to one thought. I wonder whether I understand enough about people to comprehend what they mean by *death* and *dead*. Creator looked at Singer and could only think, Here, in this one fraction of a second of this video, he is already dead. God knows how or why, but he is dead. And I've done exactly what Specht asked, the very first thing he asked, here in the studio.

Do you also work from death?

Creator switched off the projector and ejected the video. Fuck you, Specht. What have you done to me? I heard Creator say that now, hissing. What kind of sick dirty game were you playing with me?

At that moment, his phone tinkled; it was lying on the big table as well.

Hello, he said, terrible quietly.

Whoever it was on the other end of the line, their voice came from another universe; that was obvious.

Hi, sweetheart.

For a moment, he lowered the phone as if he could hardly hold it, then clamped it against his chest.

No, he said, pressing it against his ear again. I'm already up. No, nothing. Nothing's going on. It's just terribly windy. You're incredibly early. It's — oh, is it that late already? Is something wrong?

I could see that Creator was, at this moment, making the greatest effort he'd made in his whole life.

He started listening. If I'd listened very closely, I might have been able to hear Lidewij's voice, but I could never have made out her words, not with this storm raging around Withernot.

Induced, I heard him say.

Lidewij explained what that was, as if that was necessary—he'd already understood. The child had to be born now, today, soon. Lidewij had had contractions in the night; she hadn't gone into real labour, but even though she had more than a month to go, they had to play it safe—that was what the doctor said. The contractions were being artificially stimulated right now—they were inducing labour. It was definitely best for the birth to be as natural as possible, but if complications arose they'd have to operate.

A caesarean? I heard Creator ask.

Lidewij was obviously trying to reassure him; she was getting them every ten minutes now, massive contractions.

A centimetre, Creator repeated. One centimetre dilated.

Now I heard, right through Creator's eardrum, a cry.

Breathe, Creator shouted. Just breathe calmly.

He took elaborately audible calm breaths for at least a minute.

When that was over, he said, Honey, I'm going to get dressed straightaway.

I don't know why he said that. I think for a moment he really imagined that he was just up, in his pyjamas, in a life in which only this one birth would take place.

Hang in there, honey. I'm on my way.

And he clicked off the phone.

That was ten minutes ago.

After that, I didn't see him look left or right. He was all go. He opened the sliding doors and ran out into the garden. A wave of air rushed in, the popping paper flew up, and the print and the photos blew off the table. He grabbed some wood from the lean-to next to the sunroom — dry brushwood that Lidewij had collected in the birch wood in autumn. At the end of the garden, by the reed border, he built a pile. He got a plastic bottle of turps from the studio and poured it over the branches, but after that he couldn't find matches anywhere in Withernot, until he found a box in the drawer with the pencil stubs and ran back out with it. The fire flared up like an explosion, spraying sparks with what sounded like an enormous sigh. Creator threw another armful of branches on the flames and ran back into the studio. From everywhere he grabbed the prints, photos, videos, and even the cheque for fifty thousand euros to throw on the fire, which was now as tall as him. For a moment, his body was silhouetted black in front of the roaring flames.

From where I am now standing, I can see him out

of the corner of my eye. For a second, I even thought he would throw himself in the flames — it was blazing so high, and he is that small. My God, what a nondescript figure he cuts, and now he's turning around … not for me, but to rummage through the basket with the paint rags, getting out the black plastic bag with the untouched videos — what have they got to do with it? — but he still takes them back out into the garden. As he walks back again, there is a stench of poison, the flames consuming the videotapes take on a garish, green colour … he's still going to go back one more time …

That's it then, this is what my presence in the world comes down to. Supporting the image of someone I will never know, who will never see me. Being made on commission for someone who died before he could come to pick me up. Never seeing anything more of myself than my reflection — the strangest, least fathomable picture to come my way, yet nothing more or less than what I was.

I, an artefact, shaped by human hands, made for human eyes.

People are more scared of death than we artefacts. That has become very clear to me. If you add a thousand fears to my fear, you'll come close to understanding human fear. I don't know what I owe this realisation to — I'm not human, and I'm about to go up in smoke. Why did I have to know? That it's beyond them, people, the thing that is about to happen to me? Having disappeared is beyond them.

Whoever Specht was, he hadn't been able to accept that Singer had disappeared — and he went to Creator and asked him to do the impossible. *Bring him to life*. And he called the boy his son, God knows why.

And Creator went to work, on me, on me, on maxima me.

They think they create, but they make something that can't be grasped. It eludes them; they don't know what they are creating. They bring monsters into the world, they turn us into Singers, they make a person, and then get terrified. Singer, why you, why did you exist?

Now he's standing opposite me. Creator. He smells of smoke. A capillary has burst in his left eye. He has burnt the ball of his left hand; he sucks on it. He has brushed a hand over his forehead, leaving a black smear, a streak of charcoal.

Why? Why do I have to be destroyed?

What kind of incomprehensible danger is Creator in because of me?

Everything that referred to me, everything on which I could be seen, everything that could prove that I existed, everything has to go …

So this is it, here in front of me—the man who doesn't want me to exist. I mustn't exist; I must never have existed. If I exist, he is in danger. I can see him thinking that; it's him or me, me or him … how can this be possible? How can Creator possibly want to kill me? Will the hand that made me be the hand that kills me?

He spreads his arms, but isn't wide enough to reach

from right to left. He bends, grabs my upper and lower stretchers and, lifting, turns me on my side. Now I am standing—but head down. He clamps me against his body. He can't see a thing with me up against him like this; he wobbles like a dancer with a dead partner slumped over him.

Something happens that Creator, with me blinding him like this, can't know. But I feel it. Something behind me, something clamped between my linen and my frame, lets go of me. It was only just perceptible: something let go and floated irrevocably away from me.

And so he wobbles out of the sunroom, hugging me, stumbling over the step of the sliding doors. I fall back-first onto the cold grass. Swearing, he picks me up and manhandles me over the lawn, and I feel the approaching heat on my back. His mouth presses against my stomach, or is it my middle, twenty centimetres to the right? He stumbles on, two more steps, and lets me go ...

It didn't hurt; that's not it. When it comes to suffering like a human, there are other stories that go deeper and are immeasurably truer. There was just as much fire as is necessary to make an Extra Fine Quadruple Universal Primed of two by one twenty go up in smoke. I toppled backwards into the heat. My canvas caught fire before the stretchers, the wedges, the cross. I crackled because I was as dry as a bone. I thought one flimsy thought: He hasn't even signed me. And I became, yes, a shower of sparks, I imagined that clearly while feeling the paint melt and seeing Creator stare, upside-down, for just a couple of seconds before turning away. My frame was glued, all of three point six, the wood of the cross, too, that must have burnt for quite a while, but I became a shower of sparks and my sparks became flakes of ash, a large spark becoming an especially large flake, which floated over Creator who was walking slowly back to his studio. It drifted through the garden like a snowflake that has lost its flurry, and I descended, on a strangely calm gust of wind, back into Withernot. I think Creator saw me. He followed me with his eyes and must have seen me coming down — all things considered, almost like a feather — a good distance inside the studio, and I landed on the back of a Polaroid.

Hurrying again, he walked over and picked me up. Not as a flake.

That was something I was immediately incapable of imagining anymore.

Fuck, he said, and looked. More to the point, I felt myself being picked up and turned over and torn in two. Then he looked at me, and I looked back, and I realised what I had felt when something had let go of me so mysteriously. The Polaroid! The Polaroid of me.

It wasn't that I suddenly felt small. On the contrary, I was as wide as ever. I was myself in every detail, except I was no longer the canvas—I was the reproduction of myself, the only one, and I existed, yes, I did, I existed like the face on the shroud; torn in half as I was, I existed, like Lidewij's mother on the rim of the last glass.

I was sure that I would be torn again in the other direction, and then again, and thrown in the wastepaper basket, but that didn't happen. Creator looked at me, my minuscule eyes exchanged a glance with his, and he closed his eyes, as if hoping he was dreaming, and finally put me in the breast pocket of his shirt.

FIVE

What I'm going through now is indescribable. Besides the tear, which has turned me into two halves, slipped one behind the other in Creator's left breast pocket, so that I've actually become two snippets, I now have to cope with a deep, regular beating sound as well. I have ended up with my picture against Creator's body, in sweaty darkness, and it's like my ear is pressed against a big drum. Every second I hear a boom, sometimes quickened, and there's also a kind of bellows. That's the word for it, bellows, and my world now moves up and down with heavy rustling.

To my astonishment, Creator took his bike rather than the van after running into the front garden. Later, I would understand why. Close to the gate of the track they call the drive, the storm had uprooted a tree, dumping it right across the garden and the path. While Creator dragged his bike over the tree, the rustling grew heavier, and the booming less regular and more desperate.

I had never been this close to a body before. It's bizarre; I've had to lose my canvas and my entire frame to get close to someone's skin. I start to understand it a little, what it's like to be made of flesh and to breathe, to have a heart that harries you as if you were a ship riding a storm. How can people bear themselves? Besides sweat, I also caught the occasional smell of the woods. The wind died down, but now and then I clearly felt a chill on my outside back from the gusts of damp morning air.

I must have covered this route in the reverse direction when I was still a canvas and unpainted, in the van, but all I remember of that is bumping through a summery forest and having a stream of patches of light projected on my white surface through the leaves that were sliding by. Then, it was like being carried off by a lover. Now, I could only think one thing: This is not what I was made for, to move like a human. I'll never survive it.

I don't know how long the bicycle ride through the woods and suburbs lasted, but when we reached Lidewij in hospital she was already three centimetres dilated, and the contractions were coming every three minutes. It's a question of hours now, a female voice said. She pronounced her Rs in the back of her throat and had a sing-song voice. The contractions are starting to really come now — it's good you've made it.

Creator was still panting — he had started cycling faster and faster — and now tried to breathe along when a contraction came. He had, I presume, sat down next to the bed. I got the impression that a contraction was something that hurts.

There was someone hanging on the wall in the room; at least I heard Creator say something about a print of water lilies and a pond. That was after a while, when he'd got more or less used to the rhythm of the recurring contractions. He was looking for a subject with which to distract Lidewij in the intervening minutes.

That could have been me, I thought, feeling a gulf of regret. I could have been a glossy Monet print, and spent every day of my entire life attending human births in a regional hospital.

Immediately after entering the room, Creator had bent over to kiss Lidewij.

You smell of smoke, Lidewij said.

Creator said he had lit a fire.

Just like that, first thing in the morning, in your pyjamas?

Waste paper, old sketches, paint rags, Creator said.

Weird, he added, after a silence. I woke up this morning wanting to get rid of the junk.

You must have felt it coming, Lidewij said. Typical.

Then she started groaning, and Creator breathed demonstratively through his lips, and the rustling around me sounded like a judgement. When the contraction was over, a silence fell.

Baby's presenting perfectly, said the voice with the throaty Rs. Head first, just like it's supposed to be.

She left the room humming.

That was a whopper, Lidewij said. They're getting stronger each time.

She grabbed Creator's hand, but he said ouch.

Scorched, he said. It suddenly flared up, because of the wind.

A silence fell.

You've got a smear there, Lidewij said. It felt like she was trying to wipe Creator's forehead with her sleeve.

Did that journalist call?

Minke Dupuis? He was playing for time, I realised that, as if his life depended on him doing his best to make everything that wasn't happening here, in this room, at this moment, seem unimportant. He was hoping to make it to the next contraction without answering; he was hoping to keep the truth out of the birth of his child.

She's still on my hand, Lidewij said. Look, the number of her mobile.

The next contraction was a long time coming. I heard a high-pitched hiss, presumably from a machine.

I had the weirdest dream last night, Lidewij said. That he was born.

He?

Yes, he was a he and he was born and I had to ride a trishaw to Withernot. You were already home and I rode through the potholes on the track and kept shouting out, hold on, and then there was a specially deep pothole and I thought, I've bounced him out, out of the trishaw behind me, and I looked back—here comes another one.

Lidewij started to groan, and Creator started to pant.

That was just a little one, Lidewij said. That's no use to us.

In the darkness inside Creator's pocket, her smile suddenly appeared before me.

And then? Creator paused. You looked back and then?

Then Singer was sitting there. In the trishaw. The size of a baby, but still absolutely Singer.

And then? I could feel Creator's heart pounding. I felt the passion with which he wished the dream had ended there.

Lidewij hesitated, then said quickly, Then I woke up with the first contraction. Not as strong as now, but still. Weird.

Yes, weird.

I think Creator went to kiss her, but Lidewij said something else.

Do you know what I thought when I was awake—

I relaxed through the first contraction and I thought, If this is a job someone has given me and I've been crazy enough to accept it, then I can't give it back anymore, not even if I wanted to, not now.

The woman with the voice had come back; silently, she checked the machines Lidewij was hooked up to.

Look, she said to Creator, that line's its heart. Just fine. But it mustn't come under here.

She disappeared out of the room again, evidently having shown Creator where the line had to stay above.

I could tell from his breathing that Creator wanted to say something. It was as if, on hearing Lidewij use the word *job*, he had made a bold decision, complete with a deep sigh and a suck of air into his lungs.

Lidewij, he said, in a voice that seemed deeper. It's a strange thing, by the way, how a voice resonates in a chest and makes it all tremble. These mortals are made of unusual material.

Lidewij, Creator said, there is no Singer anymore.

He jumped, his heart missing a beat, from her reaction. She'd said, Oh God, and it had come out as a groan. Oh God, I knew it, I dreamt it.

Creator took another deep breath.

Singer's been picked up, he said.

Picked up? Why didn't you say so? Lidewij was relieved; I could hear that in every word. Picked up, she repeated.

Who by?

The guy from the phone call, Creator said. From the four-wheel drive. You know, the one who rang six months ago, when they didn't come to pick him up.

And?

And what?

What was his reaction?

Oh. I don't know. Beautiful — he thought it was beautiful. And looked just like him.

And Specht?

Creator hesitated. Somehow he couldn't bring himself to say what he had heard from Minke that night — that Specht was dying.

Specht will be satisfied. That's what the four-wheel-drive guy said. More than satisfied. Specht couldn't come. Apparently he's ill.

Seriously?

No idea.

Poor Singer, Lidewij said. If only he's not too late.

He's only paint.

Don't say that. You put your heart and soul into it.

Another contraction was on its way. Lidewij waited it out in total silence, and Creator hardly breathed along. When it was over, I heard nothing for a while and then sobbing.

Hold me, Lidewij said.

Creator bent forward and laid his right arm over Lidewij's chest.

Hush.

Lidewij's sobbing sounded insanely close, as if her breath was fanning me inside Creator's breast pocket. But it wasn't sorrow I could hear. It was something else. More frightening than sorrow.

It was such a horrible dream, she said. Horrible. I looked into the back of the trishaw, and Singer was sitting there and Singer was dead. I'd been riding through the forest for hours and he'd been dead the whole time.

Now she was crying with long, howling gasps.

Hush, Creator kept saying. Hush now.

In that instant, the voice of the woman broke in, swearing and sounding high and shrill.

I told you! If the line comes under here, you have to tell me!

Somewhere down the corridor a buzzer went off. Creator had let go of Lidewij, footsteps approached, the door to the room swung open.

A man asked, How long since we've had a signal?

No signal? Creator said in a monotone.

What is it? asked Lidewij. Is something wrong?

Page Verdurmen, said a male voice. He's still in the building.

Footsteps went off, others came in, Creator was pushed back to a corner of the room, machines were disconnected. I don't know if Lidewij had another contraction during the consternation, but they wheeled her off, and Creator started moving, out into the corridor, following the bed, his heart banging like a hammer.

I was there through those last anxious hours before an exhausted surgeon came to tell Creator the outcome and stammered while trying to decide what to explain first — about Lidewij or about the child — but I only remember the pounding of Creator's heart and the uncontrollable waves of his panicked breathing. It was obvious that Lidewij had disappeared through the double doors of the operating theatre. Now and then, Creator left the hospital for a short walk through a wood. He talked to himself. It was like the way he talked when he was working on me — How long ago now? — but he wasn't talking to me, and it sounded like he was constantly asking questions. Why? Why? Why? I heard him say, almost roaring, and suddenly I even thought I heard him shout out *Mercy* or *Spare me*. Goodness, how could I think of anyone other than Specht, but I didn't have the slightest impression that Creator was still capable of making any kind of connection. It was actually a mystery to me where his words, when he actually spoke them, were going. What on earth are they doing, people, when they call out things like that — stand by me? Who are they addressing?

Only a few thoughts were pounding through my head. I didn't exist anymore; that much was clear. But I was still the last person in Lidewij's thoughts before she disappeared into the operating theatre. *I rode through the forest and the whole time Singer had been dead.* I repeated the words as a kind of mantra. I had been torn in half and I was still Singer; I sat in the back of the dreamt trishaw and my mother looked back. I had no choice. What else could I do but cling to that possible backward glance? Mummy, Mummy, look back, for God's sake, look back, let me exist — I'm here after all, even if only in Lidewij's sedated head, even if I'm being torn and blacked out of my creator's thoughts, even if I'm a rattling corpse in the back of the dream of a woman under anaesthetic — look back, look back …

Who am I when she sees me?

What kind of fate is this, never being able to know who I am unless someone is looking at me?

Who will see me, please? Who will make me exist?

It must have been late in the morning when Creator saw the double doors opening in the hospital corridor and heard that he was the father of a son.

An eighth-month son.

Details of size and weight followed, but Creator didn't hear them. He only asked, My wife, how is my wife?

We've got your son in the incubator now—we'll have to monitor him for the time being, said the surgeon. You can see him in about a quarter of an hour; unfortunately, it will be through glass for a little while yet.

Only then did he answer the question.

Your wife.

The surgeon took a deep breath and wiped his forehead.

Still unconscious, but out of danger.

You could hear that it was a sentence he'd said before.

A groan welled up in Creator, and I heard it coming from very close quarters, rumbling deep inside before it rose up and left me shaking.

He had seen Lidewij lying there, unconscious, as the surgeon had said, in a room full of equipment.

He had whispered, Fearless Fly, while kissing her on the forehead.

He had gone to the maternity ward where the incubators were and stared through a window at a stark-naked baby. It breathed as if drinking slugs of liquid air.

A boy—that was very, very obvious.

Stijn, he whispered.

I didn't comprehend any of this until later, when Lidewij had returned to Withernot with Stijn, which was indeed the name they were going to give their son. Whopping great balls, Creator then said.

He left the hospital mid-afternoon, but didn't ride home—at least, not straight home. He rode in the opposite direction, through Laren, to the endless bicycle path that separates Utrecht and North Holland. He cycled calmly, and his heart and breathing were calm, too. The wind had died down. Branches that had been torn off in the night were scattered over the path. Past the White Mountains, workmen were cutting up a fallen beech; I heard the roar of chainsaws.

They were still audible in the distance when Creator got off his bike. He knew this place. He leant his bike against a tree and walked to another tree. He did something very strange to that tree, which I felt very clearly. He pressed himself against the trunk, first his head, as if pressing his ear against someone's chest, and then his whole body, as if hugging the tree. It felt rough and barky.

Only then did I realise that the big jolts I was feeling weren't coming from outside, from the tree, as I had thought for a moment. They were rising up in Creator himself, from his diaphragm. Creator was crying. And while crying, he let himself slide down the tree he was holding tight, bending his knees and finally rolling over on one side. He lay there like that until the jolting lessened. Then he got up and sat down right in the middle of a mass of damp leaves with his back against the tree.

He sat there like that and pulled me out.

One after the other, us, the two halves of his making. And he laid us on his lap. Very carefully, he slid us up against each other and made us whole by looking at us.

Tijn, he said.

Where are you, Tijn?

I knew very well how incomprehensibly small I was, how minuscule the face he had worked on, picking his nose, for weeks, how minuscule my middle, millimetres to the right of the tear. I was as minuscule as a thought, and yet I looked up out of Singer and was as wide as I had always been. I think I'm expressing it properly. I looked up from Creator's artefact and was as wide as I could be, and I saw Creator's face and how he was beyond consolation. Once I had gone so far as to call it a countenance, but my face was now so small that one of Creator's tears was enough to drown it — and he wiped me dry again with his left thumb.

Singer, he said.

Where are you, Singer?

Creator looked up and around, as if we were there — Singer and Tijn and the newborn son who was going to be called Stijn.

He said all this out loud, not to me, but it was meant for me.

In the distance, the chainsaws sounded: short bursts at long intervals. There must have been a farm closer by; at least I heard a cow, once, between two chainsaws — a cow, one distinct moo, muffled, in a shed.

He stayed sitting there like that, and I suspected that the sun had sunk lower in the sky. I remembered him once telling Lidewij that two Fjord horses grazed there, in this spot close to Groeneveld Castle, with their heads at each other's rear hooves. That must have been the tearing noise I heard. And I also heard, further away, the bells of a level crossing.

What possessed him? Why did he call himself your father? Why did he want me to make you?

Another giant tear spattered my surface, this time near my feet.

The bastard, the filthy sick bastard. What am I supposed to do now? How can I go on if the world finds out what I've done? What did he do to you? Why did you have to die?

I knew what he saw when, after wiping his eyes, he looked at me again.

Me, dead.

That was what he had worked from. Death. And he hadn't seen it; he had thought me alive, even in that last Polaroid, the one Specht had given him at the last moment, trembling with an uncomprehended emotion. Even in that Polaroid, Creator hadn't seen it.

Forgive me.

He didn't say that. I thought it. I thought, How can I tell him? How can I, two halves of a Polaroid, an artefact of an artefact, tell him he didn't know what he was doing? And I realised that it didn't matter; nothing I might say if I could speak mattered. Not to him, not in this instant. I was Tijn, I was his son, I was Lidewij, I was Minke, I was everyone he hadn't seen when they were standing before him, everyone who had ever sat for him, and he should have seen how small and incomprehensibly vulnerable we are and a hair's breadth from being nothing at all.

He must have loved you so terribly much.

That's something else I don't know—whether Creator thought Lidewij's words. He looked around, and he was exactly there where Tijn had hobbled over to him with his pants around his ankles.

Not having looked.

I tried to understand it.

Not having looked, not really, not with eyes that can see. That was what his fate came down to. Having accepted the job, solemnly—Yes, really, I'll bring him to life, I'll save, I'll save ... But what had he known about it, about what it takes to be up to that task? Who are we if we look but do not see?

Stijn, he said. But he wasn't addressing the words to his son; at least, I suspected that he wasn't.

Trust me, he said. Please. I want to be worth your trust.

Understanding who people talk to when they have something really urgent to say is beyond a support.

They think there is a father—that's what it seems like to me. Even though they can't be sure he's there, they think he is. That must be it. They need someone who never ever lets them down.

There was visiting that evening, and Lidewij might have come round from the anaesthetic, but Creator rode home first, along the whole of his endless half of the path between him and Tijn and further still, to Withernot. He hummed and whistled the *Marseillaise* and *Yesterday* by turns, sometimes sounding cheerful, then fierce, and in between he shouted, Bastard, dirty, sick bastard! and so approached the gate across the track they called a drive. The tree was still lying there. I had been slid back into his breast pocket. The sun was halfway down the trunks of the birch forest on the left.

I felt an intense warmth, almost heat, take charge of Creator's body. Things started pounding and thudding around me again. Creator gasped.

He told Lidewij about it two weeks later, the day before she was allowed home with Stijn. That's why I can finish my story.

A car was parked with its nose against the tree.

The police, Creator thought instantly.

The police have read Minke's article and found Singer on the Internet on a site where you can rent boys, and now they've come to get me. I'll have to explain myself, and no one will believe me.

But it was a four-wheel drive.

It seemed to be empty. When Creator got off his bike, the driver's side window buzzed down. A bald man with an earpiece cleared his throat and said, Just in time.

Just in time, Creator repeated. He was lost for words of his own. His throat was parched.

We were about to turn back, the man said. Empty-handed.

Creator recognised the voice from the Rotterdam accent. This was the person he'd spoken to a week before Easter, more than six months before.

Mr Valery would like to speak to you.

Valery, Creator repeated. He's in the EMC, he's …

He was about to say dying, but the man with the earpiece got out and walked around the car. He pressed the boot lock, and with one sure movement pulled out a kind of rack with wheels that folded out into a wheelchair. Then he opened the car door on the other side and helped someone out. Which is to say, he bent down and carefully slid a figure out of the car and lifted him into the wheelchair.

If you would be so kind as to open the gate, the bald man said.

Baffled, Creator laid his bike down and opened the gate to Withernot.

With his chin, the bald man indicated that Creator should come over behind the wheelchair.

Do you have the cheque with you?

The figure in the wheelchair nodded.

The bald man helped Creator lift the wheelchair over the tree. No one spoke. The bald man walked back to the car and lit a cigarette. Then Creator pushed Specht onto the track with the potholes that badly needed filling. The bald man stayed behind at the car. Creator rolled Specht into the sunroom, which still reeked of smoke.

He must have had enough time while pushing the chair to take charge of the situation, but he had only stared at the back of Specht's head. More exactly: the neck as skinny as a child's wrist, the smooth head with the odd tuft of matted hair, the sharp bumps where the neck joined the skull, the downy, purple-veined ears as thin as bat's wings, the liver-spotted scalp and the distinct yellowish lump beneath it, in the place where Stijn had his fontanel.

If I as much as blew on him, I'd have killed him, he said later to Lidewij. At the moment itself, he was confused, and felt, despite the pitiable shape that Specht was in, an irrepressible nausea rising within him. Death, that was more or less what he thought. I'm pushing Death himself into Withernot; filthy, sick Death.

He put Specht in the middle of the sunroom, which was dusky and strewn with traces of the previous night.

It was as if I'd pushed him into hell, Creator said. Ash everywhere, and your green cloth and the popping paper and the bucket and the mattress.

Spare me the details, Lidewij said.

Creator definitely hadn't told her everything. From the preceding events, he had mainly left out the videos and a lot of Minke. And of—I could see right through him.

So there he sat, facing the sliding doors, next to the bucket, in a puddle of water, Creator said. The great Valery Specht.

What was the puddle doing there?

That's another story, Creator said. Specht sat in his wheelchair and I stood opposite him. And I told him that he was too late. Specht hadn't understood at first. Initially, Creator even wondered whether Specht was all there. Sometimes he seemed to doze off.

But when he spoke, his voice was still unexpectedly firm.

You violated the agreement.

Creator didn't answer.

You showed Singer to Ms Dupuis. There's no doubt of that.

Creator might have been thinking of protesting.

I presume at least that Ms Dupuis also gave you her article to read.

He still had his Rotterdam accent and the high voice of someone whose voice never broke.

Creator was surprised.

She faxed it to me. At least, it arrived at my office early this morning; my secretary brought it to me in hospital, Specht continued. The article about me. She still had that much decency. Letting me read it before it appeared in the newspaper.

Creator was still speechless.

Otherwise this wouldn't have happened, Specht said. His gesture took in the whole studio with all the flakes of ash.

Otherwise you wouldn't have burnt Singer. Would you?

How do you know about that?

My secretary walked around the house and found what was left of the fire. It wasn't hard to guess what it was for.

A silence fell.

I really am too late, Specht said. Only now did his voice sound as weak as he looked.

You believed her. You showed her Singer, and then you believed everything she told you.

It was starting to get dark in the studio. Upstairs, the central heating turned on. All over Withernot, pipes started clicking.

In the end, you believed her. Not me.

He gestured. Outside, past the site of the fire, past the reeds and past the lake, you could see the twinkling lights of the new buildings in Almere.

That's Lord Peacock, Creator said. A scraping sound had come from outside: pecking in a metal bowl.

Is it so difficult to believe? asked Specht. Was I so terribly difficult to believe? I thought ...

He gestured and let his hand, which was infinitely skinny, drop back down onto his lap. I heard the flop.

I thought I'd done it the right way. That I'd given you the commission in a way that allowed you to believe in yourself, in your great talent for bringing your portraits to life.

The last words sounded bitter.

To life! I thought you understood me. You'll be saving a life! Singer! My son!

The silence that now fell was so deep that outside, from the channel halfway across the lake, the drone of a barge was audible.

It wasn't believable anyway, Specht said. Him. Alive. That was why I told you he was dead. I shouldn't have said that. Ever. But if I'd told you what he really is, you wouldn't have accepted the commission. You would have started by asking where he was now.

Absolutely.

And I couldn't. I couldn't answer that question. That Singer had gone to, back to ...

Again, he let his hand drop to his lap.

Back to The Hague.

The Hague?

Back to his slow suicide. Back to his filthy room. Back to his life. His lies. His hustling. His heroin. His Internet site, the one he wants to blackmail me with. I really believed it, that he ... that this time he'd manage it. But he didn't trust me. He couldn't—he despised me, just like all the others, always, and he was right. I bought him. Whatever I did, it was as if I bought him. Buying was all I've ever been capable of.

I heard these words when Specht said them. I was still in Creator's breast pocket and later, when Creator repeated what Specht had said for Lidewij, I knew that they were the same sentences, word for word.

It was as if I bought him. Buying was all I've ever been capable of.

Of course, I thought of Specht's gesture here in the studio, a lifetime ago, on the feast of the Epiphany—the thin hand in the inside pocket of the far-too-baggy expensive suit, the cheque, the five figures.

And you all let yourselves be bought, Specht said. Of course you do. How could it be any other way? You, too, Felix—you only accepted the job after I'd named the price.

Creator had turned and was looking at Lord Peacock, who had turned around and was dragging his tail into the garden, heading for the site of the fire.

Innocence is the most difficult. And the most scandalous, Specht had once said.

So Singer's not dead?

Specht shook his head.

Not in the video either?

You mean Loutro.

It seemed as if each thought slipped away from Specht the moment he spoke it.

We rushed him to Heraklion by helicopter. They were able to save him, pumping his stomach and patching him up in the nick of time. That was eighteen months ago. An overdose. I found out while I was filming; he was lying there like a sleeping god … I didn't even smell the vomit next to the bed. I was just spellbound by—Christ almighty, he was so beautiful. I know what you want to say. But you wouldn't have accepted the job if I'd told you it was suicide, attempted suicide, at that moment, on the video, there, in Loutro …

Why did you want his portrait?

Creator asked the question, but knew the answer.

It was for him. Your *thing*. It would be …

Was he dozing off again?

It would be as if he was loved. Do you understand? If I was dead, who would there be to tell him that? If he got to see your thing, one day, as I knew that only you could paint it, then he would know how …

Specht raised his hand to his forehead and pinched his brow.

How much I loved him. How lovely he is. How lovely.

He cleared his throat, but stayed hoarse.

It was as if he chose me, that one time, in the compound, on the lawn.

Papa, he said. In French. He wanted to trust me. And really, Felix, later I even convinced myself ... that it wasn't inconceivable, Singer trusting life and one day taking over, not the business, but the things I found most beautiful. He loved beauty — he soaked up the most beautiful things as if it's true, that beauty really is salvation. You wouldn't believe it, but I started to dream of a window with Specht & Son on it and, inside, all of the things he found most beautiful from my collection — all the things he'd pointed out as touching him.

He ran his fingers over the light stubble on his chin, as if his hand was trying to feel that he was still alive.

Your Jeanine. That touched him.

My Jeanine? Creator was confused. That's here.

I know. But there's a postcard of it — Ms Dupuis sent it to me once, after writing a piece about my collection, to thank me.

Ah, Jeanine, Creator said.

His breathing was suddenly very calm.

Strange. Later I read that interview with you, the one in *Palazzo*. I must have felt touched because of that Pietà. What innocence, I thought. Who, today, still has the courage to paint innocence ...?

His voice rasped; he tried to clear his throat, but lacked the strength.

I'm finished, Felix, today or tomorrow. I'd just been told the day before I saw the interview with you in *Palazzo*. Ms Dupuis's.

Now he really did seem to fall asleep. Creator cleared his throat.

It touched me, Specht said. Really. It touched me more than I can say. That being your great wish — to paint a Pietà. You had even bought a huge canvas for it. Two by one twenty. For a Pietà. And when I came in here …

He pointed with a trembling finger.

It was right there, wasn't it?

Specht sought Creator's eyes. Creator evidently understood him, because he walked over to the wheelchair and turned it to face the inside wall, where I had stood for all the world to see, with the charcoal line that broke off twenty centimetres to the right of my middle. From his perspective, left. In the meantime I had become two snippets in a sweating breast pocket, but once again I felt the way Specht's piercing gaze had smouldered in my linen.

How was he? asked Specht. How did he turn out, my son — did he turn out?

Creator had already bawled his eyes out once that day, so that didn't happen again now. He fought against tears that didn't come. He sighed. I think it was the deepest sigh of his life.

Stijn, Creator said.

Stijn?

He's alive and he's called Stijn, Creator said.

And he raised his hand to his breast pocket and pulled me out.

Here, he said to Specht. I didn't keep to the agreement.

It was pitch-black in the studio when Specht finally got me in his hands.

Creator walked over to one of the floor lamps that was still standing there.

Floor lamps? Lidewij would later ask.

That's a long story, Creator said quickly.

He switched on the lamp.

Singer, Specht whispered. My boy.

He couldn't keep his hands still. I felt myself constantly becoming two parts that kept trembling back together, until he let go of me and I was lying on his lap.

You made him younger than in the video. As I'd hoped. Exactly as I'd hoped.

He thought for a moment and said, Don't blame Ms Dupuis—she only believed her own eyes. What else could she do? She only has eyes of her own, and that's what she believed with, when she found Singer's site. She didn't know what she was doing.

He fixed his gaze on me again, and I forgot that I

was torn. I forgot that I was minuscule. I even forgot that I was no longer a canvas.

You're lovely, you're so terribly lovely. There's never been anyone lovelier in the whole world.

We stayed sitting there like that, Specht and I. For minutes. Specht with his son on his lap. Me with the man who wanted to be a father bent over me. It could be my imagination, but I felt how he, without touching me, moved his fingertip over me, from top to bottom, over the tear, from left to right, from my toes to my head. And when, after an eternity, Specht looked up from me, he said to Creator, Make him. Paint him again, as he is. He's alive. One day he'll come to see himself.